A fistful of justice . . .

"You are a frisky filly, aren't you? I'm going to have a passel of fun with you," said Eachin.

"Burn in hell!" Sarah June cried, then spat at him.

"We'll see how much you change your tune . . . afterward." Roy Eachin stepped forward and began working at his belt to drop his trousers.

Slocum slid into the room like a puff of wind, moving silently. Sarah June didn't say a word, but the shift in her attention caused Eachin to spin around to see who was behind him.

"You!" he got out before Slocum slugged him. Sarah June had staggered Eachin with her earlier punch at the gate. Slocum put all his might behind this blow that started slow, built speed and exploded on the point of Eachin's chin. The man was lifted onto his toes, went stiff and fell like a cut tree in the forest.

"Mr. Slocum!" she cried. "You came back for me!"

"Quiet," Slocum said, "We have to figure how to get out of here . . ."

JAKE LOGAN

SLOCUM
TWO COFFINS FOR SLOCUM

J

JOVE BOOKS, NEW YORK

TWO COFFINS FOR SLOCUM

A Jove Book / published by arrangement with
the author

PRINTING HISTORY
Jove edition / November 2001

Visit our website at www.penguinputnam.com

ISBN: 0-515-13183-0

A JOVE BOOK®
Jove Books are published by The Berkley Publishing Group,
a division of Penguin Putnam Inc.,
375 Hudson Street, New York, New York 10014.
JOVE and the "J" design
are trademarks belonging to Penguin Putnam Inc.

PRINTED IN THE UNITED STATES OF AMERICA

10 9 8 7 6 5 4 3 2 1

1

John Slocum sat a few feet away from the roaring fire, warming his hands and listening to the talk from the half-dozen pilgrims finishing the dregs of their potent, boiled coffee.

"Yes, sir. Bonanza's the only place in all Colorado to be," declared one man with a stubbled beard and scarred face, a hard-rock miner by the look of his patched, canvas pants and faded, red flannel shirt. His hands were caked with dirt and he sported a gold tooth that flashed in the firelight everytime he turned his head and opened his mouth. "I heard of boomtowns before, but none like Bonanza."

"It's that big a strike?" asked Slocum. He had no interest in mining. He had tried that in his day and had long since decided the backbreaking labor, the danger of gas and damp and cave-in, and the soul crushing, solitary existence could never justify a few lousy ounces of gold or silver.

"Yep, surely is," the miner said. He lowered his voice and whispered conspiratorially to Slocum, "Biggest in the area. Silver. Nuggets bigger 'n your head or my name's not Samuel Larkin. I heard all 'bout it up in Denver. Why, the silver glance comes right on up out of the ground 'n almost jumps into your pocket!"

"But you haven't seen these nuggets yourself, have you, Sam?" Slocum asked. He had heard it all before. A friend of a friend said—and it was always the biggest, richest mother lode ever found. None of the men doing the talking kept it to themselves to get rich; they always bragged on it so others would rush off. If Slocum had a dollar for every "richest strike ever" and "lost Spanish treasure" and "hidden Indian gold," he wouldn't be drifting through southern Colorado looking for a stake. He would be living it up in a posh house atop Russian Hill in San Francisco looking out over the Bay, drinking Grand Monopole champagne and eating oysters and the finest foods he could buy with that wealth.

As it was, he vaguely remembered breakfast twelve hours earlier. A scrawny rabbit had been slower than Slocum and provided an insubstantial, unsatisfying meal. Without realizing it, his hand drifted to his shirt pocket where a dozen greenbacks rode, getting lonelier by the day. He fingered the outline of the scrip, then smiled.

"Where's Bonanza?" he asked.

"Mister, you jist follow us and we'll lead you to fabulous riches. The silver'll jump out of the ground and into your pocket. I swear it!" Sam was ready to tear into a hill of rock and yank out the silver right now.

Slocum grinned more broadly now. A boomtown meant opportunities other than clawing his way into the side of a mountain hunting for the vein that would make him rich. Miners flocked out of the hills at sundown to get drunk and to gamble. The whiskey helped their aching bodies and gambling made them feel they belonged to a real community as they enjoyed a pastime that had nothing to do with hard rock or assays, and everything to do with luck that might carry over to the next day's digging.

Slocum intended to take a few dollars from the miners and give them entertainment in return. If it made him richer and them poorer, that was the way of the world.

He pushed away from Sam and the other men crowded around the fire, spinning tales of riches to come, spread his bedroll, and fell asleep to the sounds of other men's dreams.

Slocum came awake a little before dawn, sneezed into the brisk air, and sat up, looking around. The miners were beginning to stir also, anxious to reach Bonanza. He had been heading for the town of Kennicut even though he had heard it was a dying town with petered out mines scarring the rugged mountains around it. Still, poking around in the soon-to-be ghost town was better than living off rabbits and other small game in the Rockies—or it had been until he had come across the band of miners going to Bonanza.

"You have the look of a man who kin read a map," the miner Slocum had listened to the night before said from where he poked through his saddlebags. Sam held up a tattered sheet of paper. Even at this distance Slocum could tell it was a crude, hand-drawn map. "Me, I'm havin' trouble makin' head nor tail of it." As if to reinforce his ignorance, Sam turned the map around and looked at it upside down.

"You need a guide to the Promised Land?" Slocum asked, feeling more alive than he had in weeks of solitary travel from Kansas. He kicked free of his blanket and pulled on his boots. Only when he had his cross-draw holster settled at his hip, the .36 caliber Colt Navy weighing it down, did he go to study the miner's map.

"More 'n Canaan. This is Heaven itself," Sam said with some satisfaction. Then his smile faded and he asked apprehensively, "This is a good map, ain't it?"

Slocum laid the map onto the ground and held the corners down with small stones while he got his bearings. He looked around, shifted the map a little, then nodded.

"We go down this canyon, take a branch to the west, and that ought to lead straight into Bonanza. Looks to be the only way, so there's no chance of getting lost."

"Yipeee!" cried the miner so loudly that those who were still asleep came awake with a start. "Let's get movin'!"

Slocum's belly growled, but there was no stopping the miner and his friends from getting on the trail right away. Slocum took some jerky from his saddlebags and contented himself with gnawing on it and sipping water from his canteen as he rode along the floor of a canyon with high, steep walls on either side. Climbing either rocky face would require block and tackle from above. Even the Utes in the area couldn't scale those sheer precipices without risking life and limb. As he rode, Slocum became increasingly wary of his surroundings.

Spring floods washed through here with a vengeance known only to nature. Any rider in the canyon would surely perish, but the bright, cloudless, blue Colorado sky told him they were safe today. No rain. And the Utes had been the friendliest of the various Indian tribes for years. Slocum had met Chief Ouray and had been impressed by the man's good-natured diplomacy and control over his scattered tribe.

The only threat they faced today was overzealousness on the part of Sam and his partners.

"Yep, yes sir, we're all gonna get stinkin' rich. My biggest problem's gonna be what to do with an entire damn mountain of silver!" Sam declared. Slocum had noted how the man hid a second sheet of paper when showing the first. That one undoubtedly revealed the richest claim around Bonanza—and had been purchased for some fantastic amount of money from a confidence man in Denver.

Still, the map Slocum had seen proved accurate, even to scale. They arrived at the mouth of the canyon leading directly into Bonanza a little before noon. But with the hot, spring sun beating down on them, revealing every little detail of the canyon floor, Slocum spotted something he had not anticipated.

He doubted the miners had reckoned on this, either.

Built across the mouth of the canyon was a man-tall, barbed-wire fence, broken only by a heavy wooden gate protected with two blockhouses better suited for military installations at a fort. Armed men poked rifles out loopholes in both garrison houses when the sentry perched high up on the canyon rim signaled them with a mirror.

A man strutted out and stood in front of the gate, waiting for the miners, his thumbs locked under his gaudy, red suspenders. He wore two six-shooters at his hips and had an arrogance about him that put Slocum on edge.

"Howdy, gents. You travelin' on through to Bonanza?" the man asked.

"Yep, we certainly are," said Sam, acting as spokesman for the group. He scowled at the sight of the rifles pointed at him. "What's going on here? There ain't no call to point them things at us. We're peaceable folks."

"Well, now, Bonanza is a fine place to be. So fine my boss figures you'd be willing to pay five dollars a head to ride on down this here canyon to get to it sometime this month. We're just here to make sure nobody tries to sneak past without paying their toll."

"What?" The miner was both surprised and outraged.

"This here is a toll road. That means you pay to use it—or you go around."

Slocum remembered the map. Not taking the toll road

added more than a week's travel to reaching Bonanza. Another canyon meandered to the northeast, then straight north where a freight road from the eastern plains went directly into Kennicut. From Kennicut across the steep mountains to Bonanza might not even be possible for all Slocum knew. Passes in this part of the Rockies tended to be high and some were impassable. Mountains topping fourteen thousand feet were common. Too common for easy travel.

"Go around!" Sam yelped like a scalded dog and slapped his leg in dismay. "You cain't make us do that! This here's a free country."

"It's a free country if you're voting and can afford the poll tax," the burly guard said. "Mr. Newcombe owns the dirt under your boots, and if you want to keep walking on it, you gotta pay."

"But five dollars!" protested the miner.

"That's in gold, either coin or dust. Don't make a difference to me. If you want to pay with greenbacks, Mr. Newcombe wants ten dollars. Paper money's not well thought of in these parts."

Ten dollars would take most of what Slocum had. He stayed away from the miners as they huddled, discussing what to do. Overheard snippets made him shake his head in wonder at how gullible a man could be. Some wanted to pool their money, get through the toll road to Bonanza, strike it rich, and then send the money back for the rest to join them, as if it would take only hours to become famously wealthy.

Finally, the resolute miner went to the indolent guard, who stood smoking a cigarette he had carefully rolled from fixings taken from his shirt pocket. Sam licked his lips and said, "All we got's thirty-nine dollars."

"There's five of you." The guard's cold glance drifted away from the knot of miners with their mules to where

Slocum stood apart. "Six if you count him."

"He's not with us," Sam said hurriedly. "He kin make his own deals. We get a discount for the lot of us?"

"A group rate?" The guard nodded slowly, as if this was a concept worth entertaining. "We let wagon trains through all the time, giving the wagon master a break. Might be I can do something for you. If you pay for four, I'll let the fifth ride free—but don't go telling Mr. Newcombe. It'd mean my job!"

Slocum knew a tall story when he heard it. Newcombe probably had no idea how much was charged for every traveler along his toll road and probably did not care as long as it was profitable at the end of the day. The portly guard with the red suspenders might pocket a dollar or two from each pilgrim as his due.

Sam hastily took up a collection and handed it to the guard, who counted it, smiled as he stuffed it into his pocket, and then thrust out his meaty hand.

"Shake, mister, and welcome to the finest damn toll road in all of southern Colorado!"

"Come on, boys. Let's get on to Bonanza so we kin get rich!" Sam never cast a glance back at Slocum as he and his friends crowded through the gate and made their way along the double-rutted dirt road leading to Bonanza.

Slocum watched them vanish—and he watched the guards. The man who had taken the greenbacks closed the gate, making a point of using a heavy padlock to fasten the chain. He signaled the guards in the blockhouses and disappeared into a smaller cabin nearby, which Slocum had not noticed before. The guards apparently lived at their post, making it all the more difficult to get by them.

Slocum found a spot to pitch his camp where he could study the guards and their routine. He had no intention of paying such a larcenous price to ride a road that ought to have been free. Bonanza seemed a better destination to him now than Kennicut, but the former boomtown was only a few days away—and getting there cost him only a few more days on the trail. If he could not tap into the riches supposedly flowing through Bonanza, he would pick up the crumbs in the other town.

Lying back against a white smooth-barked beech, hat tilted down over his forehead, Slocum watched as another band of travelers came up and dickered with the guard. There seemed to be some trouble because the driver of the lead wagon kept pointing over his shoulder at his back trail. Slocum could not hear what decision was made, but the driver paid over another wad of greenbacks before being allowed to continue. His wagon and the two with him rattled and clanked along the road Sam had taken hours earlier.

Within fifteen minutes, the *clop-clop-clomp* of a horse with a bad gait echoed along the canyon. Slocum sat a little straighter when he saw the woman leading a horse limping on a bad foreleg. She was about the prettiest woman Slocum had seen in ages. Long, nut-colored hair cascaded softly over her shoulders, framing a lovely face with wide-set brown eyes and bee-stung lips.

The rest of her was mighty appealing, too.

She led her ailing horse to the gate. The guard had already come out to open it.

This time Slocum heard what was said because the woman was shouting in anger.

"What do you mean, I have to pay? Mr. Gutherie was going to pay my way! Hasn't he come through?"

"I don't know nothing about this Gutherie fellow," the portly guard said. "All I know is that you have to pay to take the toll road. If you don't have any money, well, I might figure some way you can work off the fee." He leered.

"I'd sooner lie down with a badger! No," the woman raged, "make that a skunk!"

The guard said something Slocum missed, but the woman swung on him. Her fist connected with the point of the man's chin, snapping his head back and staggering him. He regained his balance and came for her, storm clouds of anger darkening his moon face.

"Nobody hits Roy Eachin! Nobody. Especially not some cheap whore like you!"

Eachin froze when he heard Slocum's six-shooter cock.

"Don't hit a woman," Slocum said. "You won't live long enough to regret it."

"You," Eachin said, making the word sound like a curse. He lifted his hand and snapped his fingers. "Put that hogleg down or you'll be buzzard bait." Rifles from both blockhouses poked out and trained on Slocum.

"Maybe so, but you won't be around to watch it," Slocum said coldly. "Apologize to the woman."

"In hell!"

"That's your choice," Slocum said, intending to shoot and devil take the hindmost. The blockhouses were positioned to cover the road and he stood off to one side. The restricted angle of fire might give him a few seconds to get to cover, but he had to think about the woman's safety, too. She stood squarely in front of the gate and in the line of fire.

"Wait," the brunette said, moving between Slocum and Eachin. "I didn't mean to hit you. My temper got the better of me."

"I'm not accepting your apology," Eachin said.

"She wanted yours in return, not for you to accept hers," Slocum said. He didn't feel like backing down. Eachin—and the notion of a toll road—irritated him too much for that.

"Go to hell," Eachin snapped. He stepped back, closed

the gate with a loud bang, and made a big scene of snapping shut the padlock.

"Wait!" the woman called. "Mr. Gutherie *must* have paid my way!"

"If Gutherie drove the lead wagon that came through a half hour ago, he did pay," Slocum said. "But he drove on without you."

"I told him to. I didn't want to slow them down."

"Your horse might have to be put down. You should have ridden along in one of the wagons."

"Kill Portia! I could never do that. Why, some liniment and rest will fix her right up. She's a noble horse. The best and bravest. All she needs is some care, and I can give her that in Bonanza."

"Seems about everything can be had in Bonanza," Slocum remarked sardonically. The woman looked at him strangely, not knowing all he had heard from Sam and his companions.

"Thank you for your help, sir," she said. The woman thrust out her hand like a man might. "My name's Sarah June Daniels."

"Pleased to meet you, Miss Daniels. I'm John Slocum."

She turned and stared at the closed gate and barbed wire, then stamped her foot.

"I will *not* be thwarted. I am going through to Bonanza in spite of him."

"I wish you luck," Slocum said. "Without enough money, I don't think Eachin would let his own mother pass."

"What a disagreeable man," she said hotly. "Imagine what he implied I should do to get through!"

"Many's the woman out here on the frontier who'd agree," Slocum said. "Especially a woman traveling alone."

"I am not alone. I am with Mr. Gutherie and his teamsters. Well, I was."

"I'm heading north toward Kennicut. You're welcome to travel with me," Slocum offered. He could think of many things worse than riding with such a pretty woman.

"Much obliged, Mr. Slocum," Sarah June said, "but I can't. Not with Portia's leg like it is. I'll camp here until it's better and perhaps I can talk reason into Eachin. Or Mr. Gutherie might come back to see what's keeping me."

Slocum doubted any of that would come to pass, but said nothing to Sarah June. She was a high-spirited filly and seemed accustomed to living life her own way. Such women never took kindly to advice, no matter how well intentioned.

"Then I'll be on my way." He mounted his mare and looked northward along the other canyon ending at the mouth of the toll road. It seemed to be an endless trail, but he was used to that.

"Good luck, Mr. Slocum," Sarah June called. He looked back, waved to her, and rode on, a cold, uneasy knot forming in his belly. Leaving the woman alone struck him as wrong, but he saw nothing to be done about it. Sarah June Daniels had a mind of her own and seemed determined to get to Bonanza.

Slocum followed the winding trail as it rose to merge with the trail that eventually would take him on to Kennicut. He reined back when he heard a loud scream.

A woman's scream cut through the still air along the canyon bottom. Sarah June!

Slocum wheeled around and galloped back to the toll road in time to see the gate slam shut. On the far side Eachin struggled with the fiery woman. Two riflemen moved to cover Slocum.

He froze. Slocum would die if he tried to rescue the woman.

2

"Back off, mister. This ain't your fight," one guard called from the safety of the blockhouse. He poked his rifle out farther and sighted in on Slocum.

Slocum considered his chances and saw they were slim and none. Getting plugged with a dozen rounds from the guards' rifles did nothing to help Sarah June. He turned his mare and silently headed back up the trail he had just traveled. As he rode, Slocum studied the six-foot-high barbed wire fence for any breaks. Newcombe used the toll road money well to maintain the fence.

Slocum rode to a point where he was out of sight of the guards and immediately turned toward the fence. It loomed like a giant in front of him, sharp, spiked wire points glinting dangerously in the afternoon sunlight. He took a deep breath, patted his horse's neck, and then got the mare running full speed for the fence. He knew the horse could jump. But this high?

Slocum leaned forward, putting his weight over the mare's front legs, and felt the powerful thrust upward and forward. For a fleeting moment, Slocum thought he had cut free of earth and soared like a bird. The horse tucked long legs under her and missed the upper strands of wire by scant inches. And then they thudded hard on the far side of the fence. Slocum let the mare run a dozen yards and then slowed and finally stopped to get his bearings.

The cabin where Eachin had taken Sarah June was a quarter mile off. Slocum knew he had the element of surprise on his side and had to use it wisely. He faced too many armed guards to hope to shoot it out with them and live to brag about it.

He walked his horse back toward the road down the middle of the canyon, stopping within a few yards of the cabin. Slocum uneasily dismounted and approached, aware of the two shadowy blockhouses and the armed men inside them. Then he noticed all the loopholes faced the other side of the fence. Newcombe worried about riders coming through and cared nothing about them once they had entered his private domain.

Moving more quickly now that he knew the guards in the blockhouses could not see him, Slocum went to the cabin. Even through the thick walls he heard Sarah June shouting indignantly. The woman's voice carried nothing but a tinge of anger at the moment. Eachin had not begun to have his way with her.

Yet.

Slocum glanced around to be certain Eachin didn't have a few of his men around to share the bounty that had come their way, then eased up on the latch holding the door closed. Pushing it open a few inches, Slocum peered into the dim interior. Sarah June Daniels was bound to a chair. She struggled mightily, rocking from one leg to the other in a vain attempt to free her hands, which were tied behind her. She kicked viciously every time Eachin came close, but her struggles only spurred on the man's passion.

"You *are* a frisky filly, aren't you? I'm going to have

a passel of fun with you. And you will enjoy it. You might lie about it, but you'll enjoy it."

"Burn in hell!" she cried, then spat at him.

"None of that or I'll gag you. That'd take away from both our pleasures."

"The only pleasure I'll ever have is cutting out your vile heart with a dull knife!"

"We'll see how much you change your tune . . . afterward." Roy Eachin stepped forward and began working at his belt to drop his trousers.

Slocum slid into the room like a puff of wind, moving silently. He put his finger to his lips to keep Sarah June from calling out when she spotted him.

The brunette might not have said a word, but the shift in her attention caused Eachin to spin around to see who was behind him.

"You!" he got out before Slocum slugged him. Sarah June had staggered Eachin with her earlier punch at the gate. Slocum put all his might behind this blow, which started slow, built speed, and exploded onto the point of Eachin's chin. The man was lifted onto his toes, went stiff, and fell like a cut tree in the forest.

"Mr. Slocum!" she cried. "You came back for me!"

"Quiet," Slocum said, whipping out his thick-bladed knife so he could cut her bonds. Eachin had done too good a job tying the knots to untangle them. Slocum figured that meant Sarah June was not the first woman Eachin had kidnapped with an intent to rape. The setup and opportunity out here at the end of the toll road was too good for a man like him to pass up.

"My hands are so cold," she said, rubbing them. "And the ropes cut my wrists." Sarah June went to Eachin, looked down at him for a moment, then unleashed a kick that ended in the man's ribs. He grunted and half rolled away, but did not regain consciousness. "You stinking coyote!" Sarah June started to kick him again, but Slocum restrained her.

"No time for that," Slocum said. "We have to figure how to get out of here."

"We can leave the same way you got in. Or did you pay?"

"My horse jumped the fence," he said. "There's no way she could carry two of us. The fence is too high for that."

"Portia!" she cried. "My horse!"

"Your lame horse," Slocum said coldly. "You'll have to leave it."

"No. She . . . she belonged to my pa. It's all I have to remember him by."

"Keep your memories, forget the horse," he said, growing anxious. Two guards had left the blockhouses and were poking around outside. "If we don't get out fast, we're never going to get out."

"But—"

"What horse is worth getting raped, then murdered, and left in the hot sun for the buzzards to fight over?"

"Very well," Sarah June said tartly. "If that's the way it has to be, then—"

"Can you use a six-shooter?"

"Why, yes, of course."

"Get one of Eachin's. We might have to shoot our way out of here," Slocum said. He considered riding along the toll road to Bonanza and immediately discarded the notion. He glanced over his shoulder to see Sarah June yank Eachin's six-gun from its holster. For a moment, he wondered if she was going to plug the man with his own weapon. Then she turned. From the way she held the six-shooter, he knew she had not been lying when she said she knew how to use a gun.

"What do we do, Mr. Slocum?"

"Try not to be seen, get to my horse, find a place along

the fence to cut the wires, and then get out of here."

"Why not just go on to Bonanza?" She pressed close to him. He was aware of the lush body hidden under her bulky clothing, and tried not to be distracted. "We've got this far, after all."

"There's a man with a signal mirror on top of the canyon rim. If they signaled him, they could relay a message to any guards at the other end of the canyon. We'd be trapped between two parties intent on killing us."

"But I really want to go to Bonanza," she said.

"Forget the horse, forget Bonanza—for now," Slocum said. He saw his chance and moved fast, hoping Sarah June would follow his lead. She did. Slocum left the cabin and slipped around its rough wall while the two guards were examining the gate and the padlock. One turned suddenly and looked straight at Slocum as he climbed into the saddle.

"Hey!" the guard called. "Stop!"

"Come on," Slocum said, reaching down to grab Sarah June's outstretched hand. He powerfully lifted her so she could ride behind him. Without waiting to see if she was properly seated, Slocum sawed at the reins, turned his horse, and took off like a shot. A rifle slug tore past him, and then they reached a stand of protecting trees.

"What do we do now?" Sarah June asked breathlessly.

Slocum didn't have any idea. He had hoped to find a place where the fence could be cut so they could escape. Now they had all of Newcombe's guards after them. Collecting money for a toll road depended on not letting even one rider get past. Reputation, as much as manpower, kept the pilgrims paying for the right to use the road to Bonanza.

If Eachin came to, that only made escape all the more critical. He wasn't likely to be content with only raping

Sarah June now. He would want revenge and had the look of a vindictive man.

"You jumped the fence before?" Sarah June asked as Slocum's horse struggled under the double weight. "Incredible."

Slocum veered deeper down the canyon and then doubled back on his previous trail.

"Where are you going? To Bonanza?"

"Back to the gate. It's likely to be deserted for a spell if all the guards come after us."

"What if a few remain, like good soldiers at their posts?" asked Sarah June.

"Then you'll be using that six-shooter you took," Slocum said grimly. He did not bother adding that they would both be shot out of the saddle and would be dead. If they were lucky, they'd be dead. He had seen men like Roy Eachin before and knew their cruelty had no bounds. Eachin would see that they lasted for days before they died, if he caught them.

Slocum vowed not to let that happen.

"I saw men through the trees to our right," Sarah June said. "They're still on our trail."

"Let's hope they don't spot us too soon," Slocum said. He turned right when he came to the double ruts that passed for a toll road. Straight ahead was the locked gate, two guardhouses, and cabin where he had left Eachin unconscious. Nobody stirred, giving Slocum a ghost of hope.

"Hang on," he told Sarah June. "We're going to ride like our lives depended on it." He did not add that speed and daring were their only allies. Galloping hard, the mare closed the distance to the gate. The horse's flanks lathered and her lungs heaved mightily under the strain of carrying two riders.

"John!" she cried. "To the left!"

He chanced a look at the left side of the road and saw

two guards running out, jacking rounds into the chambers of their rifles. Slocum flinched when a pistol discharged next to his ear. Sarah June had fired at the guards.

To his surprise, one man yelped in pain and clutched his arm. From the back of a galloping horse Sarah June had winged the gunman. The other guard turned in surprise to see what had happened to his friend. This gave Slocum the chance to veer from a direct path to the gate and run down the man. The rifleman dived out of the way as the mare rushed by him. Slocum had bought a few more seconds of time.

"Cover me," he told Sarah June. To his relief, she knew exactly what to do and how to do it. She began firing methodically, doing a good job of holding the guards at bay.

Slocum yanked his Colt Navy from its holster and fired repeatedly at the heavy padlock on the gate. The fourth bullet broke the lock. Slocum kicked at it with his boot, then grabbed the top of the gate and awkwardly opened it.

"I'm out of bullets, John," she warned. "And Eachin's with the others now!"

Slocum guided the mare through the partly opened gate and reached the other side of the barbed wire fence, only to remember the blockhouses and how they covered the exterior road. He lifted his six-shooter and fired twice at a rifle barrel poking from the nearest loophole. Then, with his six-gun empty, he could only ride like the wind. Bullets whined past like angry wasps until he took a bend in the road and was hidden from direct view of the guards at the mouth of the toll road.

"Are you all right?" he asked Sarah June.

"All right? I'm better than all right," she said cheerfully. "I'm with you!" The brunette laughed in delight. "That's the most fun I've had in months."

"They'll come after us," Slocum said. "I've seen men like Eachin too many times to think he will let us ride off after making such a big fool of him."

"What do we do?" she asked.

"You reload the six-shooters," Slocum said, "while I lay a false trail." He spent a few minutes erasing their tracks, doubling back and then getting some sagebrush to drag behind the mare to cover new hoofprints. He had barely finished when he heard the angry voices of men arguing.

"We can't go traipsin' after 'em, Mr. Eachin," complained one man. "Mr. Newcombe said never to leave the gate."

"Shut up," Eachin snarled. "They crossed the fence and didn't pay. Didn't Newcombe tell us to collect from every mother's son who got inside the fence?"

"But they left."

"And that woman's no mother's son," piped up another. "Surely was a pity we missed our chance with her."

Slocum felt Sarah June tense. He put a hand on her arm to keep her quiet. They were hidden by a stand of trees not ten yards from the road. If Eachin spotted them, they would be in for another deadly fight.

"She's nothing but a cheap whore," Eachin said nastily. "If we find her, you and the rest of the boys can have her as many times as you want before she wears out."

Sarah June tensed again, then looked at Slocum with her wide-set chocolate eyes. If he had ever thought brown eyes couldn't flash with fire he was wrong. But the pretty brunette kept her tongue still and her finger off the trigger of the six-gun she clutched firmly.

Roy Eachin and his men rode on down the road, lost the trail, and milled around arguing among themselves. Slocum watched and wondered if they would catch on to his simple tricks. He heaved a sigh of relief when he saw

Eachin give up and order his men back to the gate guarding the toll road.

"That's a relief, those awful men letting us be," Sarah June said. She hopped to the ground and stretched her arms high over her head. Slocum couldn't help noticing the way her firm, lush breasts flattened for a moment and then sprang back when she lowered her arms. If he was staring at her, she was returning his gaze with at least as much lust.

"What do we do now, John?" she asked.

"Wait a spell. I figure Eachin might send out a scouting party in an hour or two to see if he's flushed us. We wait until his men complain too much about leaving their safe little nest on the other side of the fence."

"Then what?"

Slocum had no answer to that. He still liked the idea of going to Bonanza, but Kennicut was almost as good and was likely to be a sight safer for him—and for Sarah June.

He dropped to the ground and slid his Colt into the cross-draw holster. Slocum reached over and took the pistol from Sarah June's hands.

"Why'd you do that?" she asked.

"It's one of my rules," Slocum said.

"Rules?"

"Never kiss a woman with a gun in her hand."

He pulled Sarah June to him, feeling her firm young body crush into his. Slocum kissed her full on those ruby lips and tasted sweet wine. He was not surprised when he found she was giving as fully as he was. Their passions matched each other as they kissed, mouths beginning to explore boldly.

Slocum's tongue found Sarah June's and tangled for a moment, then retreated. Hers chased his until they were both gasping for breath. Slocum broke off and looked down into the woman's half-closed eyes. Never had he seen a woman so delightful or beguiling. He wanted her.

He gasped when Sarah June's fingers roved over his chest, moved down to his crotch, and then gripped firmly.

"You're mighty big, John," she said playfully. "And getting bigger. Can I see?"

Sarah June did not wait for his answer. She dropped to her knees and worked to unfasten his gun belt and unbutton his jeans. As she worked down the buttons on his fly she let out a gasp of surprise.

"Big? I thought you'd be big, but not this big!"

"Too much for you?" he asked, hands resting on the top of her head. He did not have to prod her. Sarah June leaned forward so her lips engulfed his manhood. Slocum turned weak in the knees as her tongue began laving every square inch of his fleshy shaft, tickling and teasing and tormenting. Then she fastened on the very tip and gave him a tongue lashing he was not likely ever to forget.

Sarah June's hands reached around him and clutched at his muscled buttocks. She pulled his hips forward so he rammed deeper into her mouth. Her tongue raked over the most sensitive areas until Slocum felt as if he was going to explode.

He pulled back. She looked up at him, those lovely brown eyes dancing with delight.

"More?" she asked wickedly. "I'm good."

"You're better than good." Slocum said, "and I'm going to pop if you keep doing that."

"I've got a powerful hunger building inside," Sarah June confessed. "Can you do anything about that?" She pushed away from him, sat hard, and hiked her skirts as she hit the ground. Lifting her skirts high on her bare legs, she revealed a nut-colored thatch between her legs.

"You're not wearing any . . ." Slocum's words trailed off. What difference did it make, other than he didn't have to strip them off the willing, wanton woman?

He dropped to his knees and ran his fingers along the soft insides of her legs. Sarah June shivered in delight and leaned back, supporting herself on her elbows.

"Go on, John. Hurry. Fast. Do it fast and hard. That's the way I want it."

He moved into the vee of her spread legs and felt his knobbed shaft brush across her bush. He bent over, supported himself, and then shifted forward until he began poking through the delicately scalloped nether lips into her tight, moist core.

"Oh, oh, yes!" she gasped, dropping flat onto her back. "You *are* big, John. You fill me up!"

He took her at her word about wanting it fast and hard. Once he was sure he had found the target, he rammed forward as fast as he could. Friction burned at his length and spread throughout his loins like a prairie wildfire. From the way Sarah June tensed around him, he knew she was similarly possessed with the demons of lust. He paused when he was fully hidden in her tight crevice, then drew back slowly to torment her sexually.

"Oh, John, you're driving me wild," she gasped. Sarah June began thrashing about on the ground, pinned in place by his long, fleshy rod. When only the tip of his manhood remained within her Slocum slammed forward again. The rapid insertion sent new flames dancing through his body. The slow retreat and swift entry built their passions to the breaking point fast.

Sarah June brought her knees up on either side of his body and reached out to stroke his face, grip his arms, dig her fingernails into his flesh as waves of desire crashed into her. The brunette groaned, sobbed, and then arched her back to ram her crotch into his as hard as she could. She tried to take even more of his pleasuring length into her, but it wasn't possible. Slocum was already as deep into her tender body as he could go.

He reached around and clutched the fleshy globes of her buttocks and pulled hard, keeping her close as lust racked her body. She cried out, but Slocum doubted Eachin's men would hear. They had returned to the safety of their blockhouses. Then all sensible thought was driven from his mind as her body crushed down powerfully around his hidden length.

Slocum felt as if he had entered a mine shaft that collapsed around him. But no mine was ever so tender, moist, and demanding. She squeezed on his length and milked the hot flood of seed from his loins. Slocum grunted, arched his back, and pulled Sarah June to him in a vain attempt to split her apart with his manhood.

He spilled into her yearning interior and then the passion dimmed slowly like a blazing sunset fading to twilight. Slocum reveled in the feelings until he slipped from her. He sat back on his heels. Sarah June lay on the ground before him, her face flushed and a smile on her ruby lips.

So lovely, so passionate. He was glad he had rescued her.

Then she opened her eyes, and he saw the determination there not to stop. It was almost midnight before they were both too worn out to make love anymore.

3

"So?" Sarah June Daniels asked, her cheek pressed softly against Slocum's bare chest. He felt her hot breath gusting along his flesh and wished this could go on longer, with time at a standstill and both of them content. But the sun was poking up over the distant canyon rim and a decision had to be made soon about what to do.

"So you have to decide where you want to go," Slocum said. "You can come with me or you can hitch a ride on a wagon coming through, though that would be dangerous."

"Dangerous? Why?"

"All the traffic we've seen has been going toward Bonanza. That means any new pilgrims are likely to be going there, and you'd have to get past Eachin at the toll road gate."

"Or I can go with you to Kennicut?" Sarah June asked dreamily. She sat up, her naked breasts swaying seductively. Slocum saw the way the look on the woman's face changed subtly and knew the time for passion was gone. She had turned calculating, and anything they had enjoyed was past. For the moment.

"You're welcome to come along. If you decide to head back down the canyon, you'd have to do it on foot."

"Portia," she said with a deep sigh that both fascinated and frustrated Slocum. "I hate to leave such a fine horse with a lout like Eachin."

Slocum kept his peace. The horse's fate was not the least bit important when it came to deciding human lives, but saying this would only irritate Sarah June.

Slocum saw the expression on the woman's face brighten and knew he would find out what idea struck her. She started to tell him, hesitated, got her wits about her, then let it all out in a rush.

"The next wagon that comes by, John. We get into it. We *sneak* onto the toll road and get to Bonanza that way."

"What about my horse?" he asked.

"Oh, without the saddle, which of those fools with Eachin could ever identify your horse? And Eachin won't remember one mare over all the others he has seen."

"Not like Portia," Slocum jibed. Sarah June ignored him and rushed ahead, telling him her harebrained scheme. "We hide in a wagon, get to Bonanza, and then we can do what we wanted to there!"

"What were you going to do in Bonanza?" he asked.

"Why, I'm going to open a saloon. In a boomtown, this is better than owning a gold mine. You get the money from all the mines that way."

"You have the money for that?" he asked.

She looked at him, then lifted her hands to cover her breasts as if she had just remembered she was still naked. Sarah June tried to look coy and failed.

"Why, John, it's not nice for a gentleman to ask a lady such things."

He had to laugh.

"All right. We'll see what it takes to get to Bonanza, though it might be easier going to Kennicut and working over the mountains from there instead of using New-combe's road."

"Oh, that's not possible. Not easy, at any rate," Sarah June said, getting dressed slowly. She made even putting on her clothes a sensual process that kept Slocum capti-vated. "The deep canyons and mountains prevent it, until a bridge is built to Markam Pass across a really deep gorge. Then they might actually run a railroad line into Bonanza. When they do, it will blossom into a huge town."

"Until the silver plays out," Slocum said.

"Before that happens, we can get rich."

"We?"

"Why, you're going to help me with the saloon, aren't you? Unless I'm seriously wrong, you are a fine gambler. Just what the Tons o' Gold Saloon needs."

"That's the name of your saloon?"

"That's the name and that's what I—we—will make," she said, so confident that Slocum almost believed her.

Slocum peered out from under the tarp covering the last wagon in the long line of eight wagons slowly passing through the gate guarding Newcombe's toll road. Sweat trickled down his face, as much from nerves as from the heat of the day. He and Sarah June had waited almost a week for a supply train to come by. The wagon master had been more involved keeping a damaged wagon rolling and had not noticed it when Sarah June had slipped into the last wagon, Slocum not far behind.

He worried about his horse placidly clomping along, tethered to the rear of the wagon. The wagon driver had to notice sooner or later, or the wagon master might won-der where the extra horse had come from. But Slocum would cross that bridge when he came to it. Right now it appeared as if they might actually get through the fence and onto the road to Bonanza without being caught.

"I want to see," Sarah June whispered.

"Stay down," he warned. Slocum dropped the edge of the tarp as Roy Eachin strolled along the line of freighters, poking and prodding as he neared the last wagon, where Slocum and Sarah June hid. Slocum touched the ebony handle of his Colt Navy, ready to draw if Eachin exposed them. But the man stopped before he got to them.

"Let 'em through," Eachin bellowed. Almost immediately the wagon lurched and creaked forward. Slocum stayed on pins and needles until the wagon had been rattling over the rutted road for almost twenty minutes.

He motioned to Sarah June. It was time for them to reveal themselves to the driver and maybe the wagon master. He slipped forward past the boxes in the wagon bed, worked his head out from under the tarp, and scrambled up into the driver's box.

The young man driving jerked upright and stared wide-eyed at Slocum.

"Where'd you come from?" he asked after he got his wits back.

"We sneaked in," Sarah June said, coming up behind Slocum.

Slocum almost laughed at the young man's expression seeing such a vision of loveliness rising from the back of his wagon.

"You mean you've been in my bed and I never knowed it? Well, golly, the rest of the fellas'll never let me live that down." He grinned foolishly.

Sarah June sidled closer, pressing her leg intimately against the driver's.

"Don't tell them. Or if you do, why, I wouldn't mind if you exaggerated just a mite. I wouldn't be *too* embarrassed, no matter what you said."

Slocum let Sarah June work her magic with the young

driver. Within ten minutes she had the man agreeing how
terrible it was that Malcolm Newcombe actually charged
to use a road and how it was nothing short of treason that
he wanted to keep a beautiful woman like Sarah June
Daniels out of Bonanza. Slocum missed what tall tale the
brunette spun to help the young driver reach that conclusion, but it didn't matter. He figured he could have talked
the boy into letting them ride along, no matter what. On
the frontier, life ought to be free. It was hard enough
without having to pay to use a road. Cheating the toll road
owner would seem a grand adventure after a few miles,
but Sarah June got him to that point within minutes.

"So you'll let me drink free at your saloon?" the young
man asked.

"The first drinks'll always be free for you, Abel," Sarah
June said. The driver beamed at such largesse. Slocum
settled down to study the canyon and saw how difficult it
would have been trying to avoid Newcombe's toll road.
The walls were both steep and rugged, affording few
chances for a path to the rim. Anyone trapped in the narrow, winding canyon was at the mercy of armed guards
at the toll road gate.

"What's that?" Slocum asked, suddenly alert. He
pointed to a flashing signal mirror from the canyon rim.

"Don't rightly know," Abel said. "I reckon Mr. Jessup'd know. He's the wagon master and 'bout the smartest
man I ever seen."

Slocum stood in the box and tried to get a better look
at the lead wagon.

"It's stopped," he said. Slocum's heart pounded faster.
Had Eachin found out he and Sarah June had sneaked
past? With the sentry points along the canyon rim someone with binoculars might have spotted them. It was too
incredible that they could have been recognized from such
a distance.

"Whoa, whoa!" called Abel, reining back on his team. The wagon creaked to a halt. Abel fastened the reins around the brake and jumped down. "You folks kin stay here. I'm gonna see what's wrong."

Sarah June waited for Abel to get out of earshot before asking Slocum, "Did Eachin find us out?"

"I don't see how," Slocum said. He squinted into the sun trying to make out the reason for the blockade ahead. Then he made out the outlines of another fence and the long, dark shadow cast by a guardhouse.

"Get the horse saddled," he said to Sarah June as he hopped down. "We might have to make a run for it."

"What's wrong. John?" she asked anxiously.

"I'll find out." He settled the six-shooter at his hip and went to see why the man Abel had pointed out as the wagon master, Jessup, was arguing so with two armed men at the gate leading from the canyon.

Slocum figured out the problem before he reached Abel's side. The young teamster stood with fists balled and his teeth clenched.

"They want us to pay to get outta here!" Abel told Slocum. "That's highway robbery!"

"Now, it's not my fault if you didn't ask what the rules were back at the other gate," the man with the shotgun told Jessup. He was as arrogant as Eachin. "Mr. Newcombe requires an exit fee. Sort of an entry fee to Bonanza since it's such a fine place to be. You paid to use the road, now you pay to get into Bonanza."

"I'll pay you by bustin' your damned skull," raged the wagon master. The short, stocky man stepped up to make good his threat, but the guard backed off and leveled his shotgun.

"I got orders to prevent violence," the guard said.

"Then you'll do well to nip it in the bud while you're still able to," Slocum said, aiming his six-shooter directly at the guard's head. The man didn't flinch, and Slocum quickly saw why. The guardhouse was open at the top, equipped all the way around with a walkway behind waist-high walls like a military fort. Three men with rifles trained on them watched over the gate.

"You don't want to start nuthin' you won't live to see finished," the shotgun guard said. But he concentrated only on Jessup and Slocum and ignored the rest of the teamsters—to his detriment.

"Fire!" yelped one of the guards on top of the guardhouse. Curls of white smoke twisted and turned fitfully as they rose. The guards quickly abandoned their posts.

"What—" The guard with the shotgun showed signs of losing his nerve.

"My boys just found how dry it is here," Jessup said. "I tell 'em not to smoke them stogies they favor, but they don't listen. Just like I tell 'em not to use damned fool guards for target practice."

The guard swallowed hard and backed off, looking at the flames licking up the sides of the guardhouse and then to the six-gun held in Slocum's steady grip. The man lowered his shotgun and fumbled to open the gate.

"Much obliged," Jessup said to Slocum. The wagon master did a double take when he realized he had never seen Slocum before, then shrugged it off. He had a wagon train to get to Bonanza and wasn't interested in mysterious gunmen helping him along the road.

"You sure are good with that six-gun," Abel said to Slocum as they returned to the last wagon. "Reckon that's why you and Miss Sarah June make such a fine pair."

"What do you mean?" Slocum asked.

"Why, she said you and her was owners of a saloon."

"Who am I to argue with a lady?" Slocum said, shaking

his head. He settled down with Sarah June between him and the driver. They rumbled through the gate, past the smoldering guardhouse and started up the steep, rocky road leading into the mountains around Bonanza.

4

"Isn't that about the prettiest sight you've ever seen?" Sarah June Daniels asked, hands on her flaring hips and a glow to her that rivaled when she and Slocum had made love. But this time she had no eyes for him. Sarah June stared at a tattered patchwork tent flapping fitfully in the stiff breeze blowing off the Rockies.

"It is," Slocum said, but he was looking at Sarah June and not at the brand-new Tons o' Gold Saloon. They had bought the canvas for the tent as scraps from a dozen different miners and had hired the only two seamstresses in town to sew the segments together while Slocum worked as carpenter to nail together boards for a passable bar.

"Abel decided to stay and not go back to Pueblo with Jessup and the other freighters," she said. "So I hired him as barkeep."

Slocum nodded absently, his gaze moving from the lovely woman to the hills beyond Bonanza. Tailings dribbled like oozing wounds from the dozens of silver mines along the slopes. For a strike as rich as Bonanza's, there ought to have been ten times the number of mines boring into the rocky grade. Malcolm Newcombe and his restrictive toll road throttled the potential flood of miners to town and stifled the local economy.

Still, Slocum saw there was plenty of money to be had. The Bonanza strike was everything Sam Larkin, the miner he had met on the road, had bragged.

"Ready to open?" Sarah June asked.

"I've got a deck of cards, you've got the whiskey," he said. "There's nothing more we need to do other than let the miners in to spend their silver."

Slocum had been impressed by the no-nonsense way Sarah June had set about opening the saloon. She had found a supply of grain alcohol and had set to making whiskey. The few cases of tarantula juice Jessup had brought with him in the shipment where they had stowed away had lent an air of quality to the bottles of crudely manufactured trade whiskey lined up behind the bar. Glasses ran the gamut from jelly jars to Mason jars and tin cups. It would be up to Abel to pour a fair shot without giving away their profits.

Sarah June's profits, Slocum reminded himself. She had made it clear from the start that they were business partners now. She put up the money and ran the Tons o' Gold, and he was responsible for running the gambling and keeping the peace. He kept what he made off the gambling and all the profits from the rotgut went directly to Sarah June. Moreover, she had decided that business partners did not sleep together.

That didn't remove her appeal to Slocum. If anything, it increased it.

Slocum jumped onto an overturned empty dynamite crate and bellowed, "Come on in to the Tons o' Gold Saloon for a free drink!" The clarion call echoed across Bonanza and along the mountain slopes. For a few minutes Slocum thought he would have to repeat the invitation. Then he saw a steady line of men coming down Bonanza's dusty main street, intent on the canvas tent and the promised free booze.

"Come on in, gents," Sarah June greeted. More than one stopped to get an eyeful of the new saloon proprietress, but the lure of whiskey to wet their whistles kept them crowding into the tent.

"Step on up. Free whiskey. The first shot's on the house!" called Abel, enjoying his job behind the bar.

Slocum saw there wasn't likely to be much trouble until the miners got liquored up, so he sat down at a table and fanned out the cards in front of him. It took less than a minute to fill four more seats around the table and get a lively game of five-card draw poker started. The miners were as Slocum had hoped, more energetic than adept at gambling. In two hours he was more than a hundred dollars to the good and was thinking of hiring a faro dealer to entice the hard-rock miners to buck the tiger.

The Tons o' Gold was filled and everyone enjoyed themselves without getting too boisterous. Slocum knew that could change at any instant, but for the moment he was drawn outside by the brief glance he had of a redheaded woman. She stood for the briefest instant, holding back the tent flap, as she looked over the crowd. Then she dropped the canvas shutter and vanished into the dark night.

Slocum glanced in Sarah June's direction and sighed. She was a lovely woman, and he had certainly enjoyed their time before sneaking past Eachin to get to Bonanza. Once here, though, Sarah June had become a complete businesswoman and insisted they not mix profits with sex. Slocum had no intention of staying forever in Bonanza, but respected Sarah June's decision, even if he did not agree with it.

They had been good together, and he was not sure the money made up for what they had lost.

He stepped from the smoky, hot tent into the biting cold of the Colorado night. Slocum looked around, wondering if he had been mistaken about the red-haired woman. His eyes stung from the thick cigar smoke and he had sampled more than one shot from Abel's best bottle, but he thought he had seen her. He looked around town and saw a ghost-like figure flitting away down the street. Slocum followed and quickly overtook the woman.

"Yes?" the redhead asked curtly, when he reached her. "What do you want?"

Slocum had expected her to show a trace of concern at being stopped by a strange man in the middle of a rough mining camp. She didn't. In her way she was as much all business as Sarah June.

"I saw you looking into the saloon and thought you might be hunting for someone."

"And you thought to help? I need no help, thank you," she said primly.

Slocum studied her more carefully. She was tall, slender, and moved like a puff of air dancing from one flower to another. Her long, coppery hair escaped from under an expensive hat and dangled across her eyes. She made an impatient gesture to push it out of her way, but it returned. She seemed to accept it as she stared at Slocum with eyes as green as his own. From her milky complexion, she spent more time indoors than out but she was no hothouse flower; not if her reaction to him stopping her as he had done was an indication. This was a young woman who was self-assured and thought herself to be in command of any situation.

"My name's John Slocum," he said. "If I can be of any help, you can probably find me in the saloon. Good evening," he said, tipping his hat in the woman's direction.

"Wait," she said, reaching out and stopping him with a light touch on his arm. "I apologize for being so curt. I am a bit out of my milieu."

Slocum said nothing. She was educated as well as pretty.

"My father sent me to Bonanza to see if there might be reason to—"

She cut off her sentence when she saw a man moving toward them with resolve.

"Miss Simmons," the man called, his fingers going to touch the brim of a hat even more expensive than the one worn by the redhead. "I wondered where you had gone."

"That is none of your business, Mr. Newcombe."

Slocum tensed and stepped back a pace, his hand going to the butt of his six-shooter. The man stalked up and glared at her.

"You're Malcolm Newcombe?" Slocum asked in amazement. "You're still wet behind the ears."

The woman laughed and tried to hide it behind a raised hand. Then she stopped any pretense of being polite and laughed openly.

"No, Mr. Slocum, this is *not* Malcolm Newcombe. That's Buster's father."

"Don't call me Buster," the young man said angrily. "You know I don't like it."

"You would not like to hear what my father calls you," the woman said crisply.

"Who might your pa be?" asked Slocum.

"He's Colonel Simmons, and he thinks he's God returned to earth." Buster Newcombe said, as if the name burned his tongue.

Slocum sucked in his breath. He stood in the presence of the offspring of Bonanza's problems—the man controlling access by his toll road—and the hope for the future—Colonel Simmons, who owned the Colorado Grand

Mountain Railroad that could open the town and break the back of the toll road magnate with cheap, quick, frequent transport from Kennicut.

"Leave me alone, sir," Miss Simmons said to Newcombe.

"Rebecca, I want you to—" Buster Newcombe reached for her, but Slocum slipped between them. He caught the man's wrist and twisted, driving Newcombe to his knees.

"She doesn't want to talk to you," Slocum said in a level tone.

"Let me go! My father'll have your ears for this!"

"He tried already," Slocum said. "Now go peacefully or you'll go in pieces."

Newcombe jerked free, got to his feet, and glared at Slocum. He shouted at Rebecca. "You'll have to listen to what I have to say sooner or later!" Then he stalked off, rubbing his wrist and muttering to himself.

"How perfectly disagreeable," Rebecca Simmons said. "Thank you, Mr. Slocum, for chasing that ruffian away. He can be so bothersome."

"Seems like the two of you have met before," Slocum said.

"It was disagreeable then, also, when we were at school back East," she said. Rebecca looked at Slocum, as if for the first time. "You handle yourself well, Mr. Slocum. Have you a steady job or might I tempt you with a position on my father's staff?"

"Doing what?" Slocum found himself grinning in spite of himself. "Chasing off the likes of Buster Newcombe?"

"Well, yes, that could be part of it, but I am more worried about his father's henchman."

"Roy Eachin."

"Ah, you know him already." Rebecca turned grim. "He is a vicious man who often exceeds his orders—and

Malcolm Newcombe is infamous for how savage he can be when conducting business."

"What is the bone of contention?" Slocum asked, although he could read between the lines.

"Because of his toll road, Newcombe controls all supplies coming to Bonanza. The silver strike is a big one and great amounts of money can be had in free commerce," she said in her lilting voice. "My father would like to make the Newcombe toll road obsolete by running a narrow-gauge railroad line across the mountains, through Markam Pass from Kennicut."

"So right now, Buster and his father profit because they control everything entering Bonanza," Slocum said, seeing trouble ahead for Sarah June that she had not anticipated. It would not be long before Newcombe demanded a hefty cut from her profits. Either she paid the extortion or there would be no new shipments of whiskey or grain alcohol coming into Bonanza with her name on them.

Newcombe might even go into business, competing with her. Whatever clientele Sarah June won in the next few days might disappear along with the whiskey if he cut off her supplies.

"Why would they strangle business in town?" Slocum asked. "Isn't it to their benefit to grab as much as they can before the mines peter out?"

"Not really. Let the miners prove their claims, then starve them out and buy up the land for pennies on its true worth. Newcombe stands to become fabulously wealthy." Rebecca Simmons pushed back the strand of red hair again, and again it sneaked past her best effort to tuck it under her hat.

Slocum saw that the best way to help Sarah June was to stop Newcombe. More than any financial benefit that might come to the saloon owner, it felt right helping Rebecca Simmons and her father against the toll road owner.

Slocum had never met Malcolm Newcombe, but if the acorn did not fall far from the oak, he had a good idea what the man was like after a quick meeting with his son.

"Did your pa send you to make the decision or are you here with railroad engineers and others who can determine how profitable it is getting that narrow gauge into Bonanza?"

"I am my father's principal business advisor. I see how valuable it is getting track to town. It will be up to the builders to determine how best to reach Bonanza."

"I wish you well," Slocum said. Bonanza would never amount to more than a personal fiefdom for Malcolm Newcombe unless the town was opened up by the railroad. It didn't matter if Colonel Simmons drove the track through the mountains or if it was done by General Palmer or any of the other Colorado railroad magnates. But one of them had to or Newcombe would prosper and the town would wither and die.

"A moment, Mr. Slocum. You did not give me an answer."

"About taking a job with you? What would you want me to do? Besides, keeping Buster away from you?"

"A bodyguard," Rebecca said, as if the idea was startling and appealing to her. From the way she looked at him, Slocum wondered what more she might want from him. Guarding her lithe body would be an enjoyable chore, especially now that Sarah June had declared their relationship to be solely business, but Slocum felt he owed the saloon owner some loyalty.

"I have a job," he told Rebecca Simmons.

"Perhaps we can work out something. You would need only keep an eye on Buster Newcombe for me, let me know his comings and goings, anything that might reflect poorly on my father's chances to bring railroad tracks into town."

"What about being your bodyguard?" Slocum asked, only half-jokingly.

"That could be a full-time job," Rebecca said in a low, husky voice. Her tongue made a quick circuit of her lips. A faint smile brought up the corners of those lips as she added, "At the very least, it could be an all-night chore. I think I would like that."

"I think I might, too," Slocum said, "but I wouldn't look at it as a chore."

Rebecca laughed and it sounded like silver bells chiming. She reached out and laid her slender fingers on his arm. The warmth curiously sent a shiver through him.

"You have such a droll sense of humor, Mr. Slocum. Under what conditions would you work for the CGRR?"

It took him a second to realize Rebecca meant the Colorado Grand Mountain Railroad.

"I can keep track of what the Newcombes, father and son, are up to. If you are alone in town—"

"I am. I see no reason to travel with an extensive entourage," Rebecca cut in. "They do nothing but get in the way of serious business negotiation."

"Since you are alone, I can make sure no harm comes to you. They are dangerous men, the Newcombes."

"And Roy Eachin," she said. "Never forget him, never turn your back on him."

"Where are you staying? At the Eldorado Hotel?" Slocum thought this was likely since it was the only hotel in town. Rebecca nodded in assent. "Go back to your room while I see what Buster Newcombe is up to."

"Report to me as soon as you find out. Please." Again her warm touch produced a thrill.

"It might be tomorrow." Slocum said. He wanted to return to the Tons o' Gold and be certain Sarah June was getting along fine. Splitting his loyalty between the two women bothered him, but he thought he was up to it.

Working for Rebecca and the CGRR gave him the chance to get back at Newcombe and his henchman, Eachin. It also aided Sarah June by auguring a new source of cheap supplies for her saloon.

"Meet me for breakfast," she said. Their eyes met and Slocum fought off the urge to kiss her. He was not sure what Rebecca would have done if he had been so bold, but the moment passed and she bid him good evening. Slocum watched as she walked off, then heaved a sigh.

Slocum wondered what he was getting himself into, then decided the only way to find out was to track Buster Newcombe and determine what he was up to.

He angled across the street, heading in the direction Newcombe had taken. Slocum saw only one ramshackle building with a light in the window and headed for it. The crudely painted sign on the front of the building declared this to be the Bonanza Transit Company. Going to the side, Slocum pressed his eye against the splintery wall and peered into the lit room.

For a moment, he saw nothing. Then a man crossed in front of his peephole. Only when the man moved away and sat at a desk did Slocum recognize Buster Newcombe. Buster appeared uneasy and fidgeted constantly. Slocum heard muffled voices, but Buster was not the one speaking. That meant at least two others were in the room with him. Slocum edged around, trying to get a better view. The crack in the wall wasn't big enough to give him the field of view he needed. Slocum used his fingers to gently pry away more wood until he had widened the hole.

He was so intent on spying that he didn't hear the boot steps behind him until it was too late. Slocum half turned at the sound of gravel crunching. His hand flashed to his six-shooter, then bright pain blossomed in his head. The light faded to black and Slocum collapsed to the ground, unconscious.

5

Slocum felt strong hands lifting him by his arms. His heels dragged in the dirt, but he could not summon the strength to fight. His head buzzed and felt like a rotted melon, ready to split open at any second. Through supreme effort of will, he forced open his eyes and fought to focus them. The bouncing came from the way he was being dragged along. Then he hit the ground hard as the hands dropped him.

"What you want done with him, Mr. Eachin?"

Slocum's heart raced. He peered up without moving a muscle, hoping to catch sight of Newcombe's henchman. If he saw Eachin, he could draw and fire before anyone could stop him. He had that much strength—and that much anger inside bubbling up like a poisoned artesian well.

"Throw him over a cliff into some canyon where nobody but the coyotes will find his worthless carcass."

Slocum almost betrayed himself when a heavy boot crashed into his ribs. He grunted but did not respond otherwise. Satisfied he was still unconscious, Eachin left. Slocum's vision had turned blurry, but he saw the man's boots disappearing in the distance. Out of range. He could never get off a decent shot, even if it would be to the man's back.

"Come on, you sack of—"

Hands fumbled to lift Slocum over the back of a horse. As he straightened, he shifted all his weight and bore the man backward, landing hard on top of him. The man wiggled and squirmed, but Slocum kept him pinned to the ground. The man twisted like a sidewinder, then surged in the opposite direction, thinking he could escape with such an easy ploy. Slocum let him get to his feet, then froze the man in his tracks with a cocked and leveled six-shooter.

"Take one more step and it'll be your last," Slocum said. His finger tightened on the trigger just because he didn't like drygulchers or their toadies, willing to throw a helpless man over a cliff to die. He relaxed a mite and got control of his anger.

"Don't shoot, mister. This wasn't nuthin' personal. I was just doin' what Mr. Eachin told me to do."

"Strip," Slocum said.

"What?"

"Get out of those clothes—all of them—or be buried in them." The man saw Slocum was not joking and began tearing off his clothes. He paused when he got to his woolen long johns. With trembling hands he finished stripping down to the buff.

"Show me where you were going to throw my body," Slocum said. He figured it had to be close-by. This man wasn't the kind to go out of his way to do much work, even when it came to covering up a murder.

"Don't kill me, mister. You want Eachin."

"I know who I want to kill, and right now you're the one looking down the bore of my six-gun. Pick up your clothes and get a move on!"

The man hopped and cursed as sharp stones cut his feet. The cold wind had turned his flesh blue by the time they reached a hundred-foot drop at the far end of Bonanza. The wind whistled up the slope and sent a chill through Slocum. He imagined what the naked man must feel.

"Over the side," Slocum ordered.

The man swallowed hard.

"Please, mister, I won't ever bother you again."

"Your clothes," Slocum said. "Throw them over the cliff."

With something approaching relief, the man obeyed. Then he stood watching in mute fascination as the wind swirled the clothing around until the night swallowed every last stitch.

"You'll join them if I ever set eyes on you again. Understand?"

"Yes, sir, yes, yes!" the man babbled. Slocum stared hard at the man a few seconds more and saw he would probably hightail it out of Bonanza the first chance he got. He knew Slocum would shoot him like a dog, but Eachin and Newcombe might do worse for failing.

Slocum slammed his six-shooter into its holster, spun, and stalked back to Bonanza and Rebecca Simmons in her room at the Eldorado Hotel. They talked for more than an hour, then he took a note from her to give to her father. Somehow, accepting the job of courier made Slocum feel as if he had put both of his feet in a bucket of concrete. No matter what he did now, he would not be able to get free.

He bade Rebecca good-bye and sought out the bustle of the Tons o' Gold Saloon. Somehow, he could not concentrate on gambling, and Sarah June's gaiety only reminded him of what he had chosen to do for Rebecca. As Sarah June closed the Tons o' Gold around four in the morning, he told her he had to leave town for a few days.

"If you feel you have to, John. Can you tell me why?" Sarah June asked.

"Business," he said vaguely. "It'll help business here. I promise that. If I don't go, Bonanza will dry up and blow away because of the stranglehold Newcombe has on it using his toll road.'

"You haven't gotten into some kind of trouble, have you?" Sarah June asked, her brown eyes fixing on the goose egg on the back of Slocum's skull. Then she sniffed like a bloodhound, scenting Rebecca's expensive perfume on him. Slocum ignored Sarah June's look of disapproval.

"I'm always in trouble, but don't worry about it. Everything will be taken care of."

"All right," Sarah June said, obviously not believing him. "But I'm holding you to the promise of getting that fine butt of yours back here to the Tons o' Gold real soon. You weren't gone a couple hours, and I missed you."

Slocum wondered if she was telling a fib or if she meant it. He got a kiss on the cheek, then she hurried off to count the night's receipts with Abel.

Slocum had spent most of his life on the trail, but had never seen such a sight before. He stood with his toes over the edge of the canyon, looking down five hundred feet. Nowhere along that stark face did he see a ledge large enough for even a small bird to make a nest, much less a spot for a man to use as a foot- or handhold. His gaze lifted to the far side of the canyon almost a hundred yards distant.

So near and yet so far. Dust billowed from two men racing their horses on the far side. Beyond them, not a stone's throw off, lay the outskirts of Kennicut, still showing signs of life although its mines were petering out. Slocum had spent two days traveling from Bonanza through rugged country and had found Markam Pass with no difficulty. The altitude made the going rough and the constant cold, spring wind on his face had turned his skin to old leather. But that part of the trip had been a snap compared to crossing this canyon.

He looked straight down again and experienced a passing bout of vertigo. Slocum had no fear of heights, but this was an especially deep canyon.

"Come on," he said to his impatient mare. "We've got to go around."

He found a treacherously steep trail miles to the south into the canyon and another up the far face and still spent the next three days reaching Kennicut.

Once in town, Slocum replenished his supplies, then found a decent stable for his horse.

"Be sure to give her grain now and then. She deserves it after the trail we've been on."

"You come from Bonanza?" asked the stable hand. "Oh, I'm not pryin' into your affairs, mister. It's just that not many come up from the bottom of Knife Canyon the way you did. The only thing on the other side's Bonanza." He sounded wistful.

"You want to go there?" Slocum asked, seeing that the man did. "It's a real boomtown."

"Kennicut was once, too. It's dyin' now. And yeah, sure, I'd go to Bonanza in a flash, 'cept I don't want to pay that bastard who runs the toll road. And I ain't *ever* backtrackin' on your trail. Too many men get themselves too close to the edge of that hell trail and go over."

"The trail was sheer most of the way," Slocum admitted. "Where's the train depot?"

"We may not have much in the way of silver left to mine from the hills around here," the stableman said, "but we got a good train. CGRR runs straight into Denver."

"Fancy that," Slocum said dryly. "Denver's where I'm

heading." He touched his shirt pocket where he carried the note from Rebecca to her father. Although she had not told him the contents, Slocum had good reason to believe the woman had given Colonel Simmons the go-ahead to build the railroad across Knife Canyon, through Markam Pass, and into Bonanza. If so, that meant new life for Kennicut and prolonged existence for Bonanza.

He would be doing a great favor for two towns—and doing Malcolm Newcombe dirty—all with one letter. Slocum liked the feeling.

Slocum bought his ticket to Denver and rode the narrow gauge through the mountains to Pueblo, then north past Colorado City and into Denver. He stared out the dirty window of the train as it rocked through the outskirts of the Queen City of the Plains, as the citizens called it. Slocum liked the city just fine, but now he had no time to indulge in the pleasures and vices offered in Larimer Square and the sporting houses surrounding it.

"Pardon," Slocum called to the conductor. "Where could I find Colonel Simmons?"

The conductor stared at him as if he had grown an extra head. The man frowned and shook his head.

"Nobody sees the Colonel," he said. "What's your business with him?"

"Can't say to anyone but him," Slocum said. "I've heard tell he has a special train where he lives all the time. Is it parked in the train yard now?"

"Don't rightly know," the conductor said, backing from Slocum. Then he stopped and said, "Let me give you some advice, mister. He's not one to do business with. He'll eat you for breakfast and spit out your balls."

Slocum had to laugh. He had faced tough customers in his day. It didn't matter to him if Colonel Simmons owned an entire railroad and had a thousand men working for him. Sometimes it was harder facing a bronco that refused to be broken or a calf that wanted nothing to do with getting branded.

"I've had dealings with his daughter," Slocum said. "I think I can handle her father."

The conductor looked baleful and turned and walked away, muttering to himself about "fools and damned fools."

Slocum was thrown forward as the train screeched to a halt at the depot. He made his way to the platform and looked around, wondering how hard it would be to find out if Colonel Simmons was tending business here in Denver or was out along the hundreds of miles of narrow gauge he had laid across the state.

"A spider," Slocum decided. "A spider dangling in a web of steel rails." No matter where Simmons might be, he would return to the center of his power and influence in Denver—here at the rail yards.

Slocum started to ask the ticket agent, then decided to poke around on his own to keep his interest from becoming common knowledge. If the conductor was in such fear and awe of his employer, a mere ticket seller might do worse than clam up. He might summon some of the bodyguards Simmons undoubtedly employed. Slocum wanted to avoid needless explanations that would keep him from returning immediately to Bonanza.

Walking around, cinders grating under his boots and acrid smoke from the engines in his nostrils, Slocum found a short train with a powerful engine in a siding not fifty yards from the depot. Three passenger cars were gilded extensively and even sported expensive, beveled, glass windows. If a wealthy man wanted to ride around Colorado in style, he would feel secure doing it on this train.

Slocum swung up onto the rear platform on the last car and knocked on the door. He heard the echo pass through the car and seemingly vanish into the next. He had the impression the engineer might jump at the sound of him knocking at the rear of the train. Slocum waited a few seconds, then knocked again. When he got no reply, Slocum tried the fancy gilded doorknob. It turned easily, and he slipped into the car.

His eyes went wide in surprise when he saw an ornate coffin sitting on a bier. The width of the large coffin made slipping by on either side difficult. Slocum rested his hand on the coffin and verified what he had suspected.

The metal was beaten gold and the shining diamond points were not mere glass—they actually were diamonds mounted in highly polished mahogany. On impulse, he opened the coffin, half expecting to find it occupied.

"I'll be switched," Slocum said, staring at the bright red satin interior. A pillow with a slight depression in it showed where a head had rested recently. A few white hairs had been left as mute reminder of whoever had been in the coffin. The rest of the interior showed similar use. A short man had pressed his outline into the satin, then had been removed—or had climbed out.

Slocum edged around the coffin, eyeing it from all angles. It had the air of being old, perhaps many years old. The mahogany wood and metal fittings had been expertly cleaned many times and showed some wear from the meticulous care.

Slocum shook his head. He didn't understand what the coffin meant, but Colonel Simmons was not in it and he had a letter to deliver. Leaving the car, Slocum stepped onto the platform between the last car and the next. He rapped sharply on the door.

This time he heard the steady click of boot heels on the floor inside the parlor car. The door opened to a smallish man with white hair in disarray and a precisely trimmed goatee. The man's appearance struck Slocum as humorous. It was as if he had been awakened unexpectedly and had not taken time to comb his hair. But it was only early afternoon and Slocum doubted the man had been asleep, especially wearing the outfit he did. The man's clothing was both expensive and impeccable, a uniform for some unit Slocum could not identify. Slocum had been a captain in the CSA and thought he had seen every possible emblem and insignia, both to salute and to shoot.

"Colonel Simmons?" he asked, finally finding a gold eagle on the man's collar tab that led him to make the assumption. "My name's Slocum, and I have a letter from your daughter."

"I'm busy. You know better than to disturb me." Colonel Simmons started to slam the door, but Slocum stepped forward and blocked it with his body.

"Here's her letter. This is mighty important or I wouldn't have come all the way to hand it to you. You *are* Colonel Simmons?"

"Of course I am, Private," the man snapped. He glared at Slocum, then gave him a once over. "What unit did you serve with?" Simmons asked.

Slocum could not determine if the uniform Simmons wore belonged to the Federals—a Zouave unit?—or a Confederate unit. Toward the end of the war, everyone Slocum had served with had worn whatever they could scrounge, irrespective of rank or origin of the cloth.

"The war's behind us," Slocum said. He had never been comfortable around men who insisted on carrying over their military rank into civilian life, possibly because he wanted to forget the horrors he had seen. The constant reminder of a uniform, even one as ambiguous as the one Colonel Simmons wore, put him on edge.

"The war's never behind us. We fight different enemies, that's all." Green eyes peered at Slocum, eyes that reminded him of Rebecca's.

"Here's Miss Simmons' letter," Slocum said. "She gave it considerable thought and thinks a rail line into Bonanza will—"

"Bonanza! Pah! A worthless place. There will never be reason to go there. What does Rebecca know of these things?"

"Isn't she your business manager? The CGRR agent?"

"Of course she is."

"I don't understand," Slocum said, wondering if the old man had all his marbles. "You haven't even read her letter. I'm sure she explains her reasons."

Colonel Simmons ripped open the letter and scanned it.

"How do I know this is from her? You might have forged it."

"It's from her," Slocum said coldly. "I'm not a liar, and I'm not a forger."

"What you are, Private, is a nuisance!" Colonel Simmons reached to a bell cord and tugged on it. From the far end of the car came three burly men dressed in military uniforms as indeterminate of unit as the one Simmons wore. "Throw him off the train, men!"

Slocum widened his stance just a mite and the three men stopped and exchanged looks.

"It's not worth dying over," Slocum told them coldly. He looked at the dotty old man and wondered how he could ever run the railroad empire he seemed to. Or was it all in Rebecca's hands or that of saner managers? Slocum didn't care.

He backed off, got through the door, and then jumped to the ground. He had done his duty and delivered Rebecca's letter. As far as he was concerned, their business was over and done. She might be lovely, bright, and a rich businesswoman, but he would not put up with her crazy father one second longer.

Slocum started back for Bonanza, fuming the entire way.

6

The trip from Denver back to Kennicut took forever, or so it seemed to Slocum. He stared at the terrain crawling by outside the rattling train but never really saw it. He was too angry at his reception by Colonel Simmons to settle down. Even after reaching Kennicut, fetching his horse and starting the arduous trip back to Bonanza through Knife Canyon did not cause his anger to die down much. If anything, the steep trail and the days-long detour only fed his ire.

He made it through Markam Pass and rode past the gopher holes dug into the mountains above Bonanza with a feeling of distance rather than expectation. The boomtown was even more active than when he had left, miners bustling about and a second general store furnishing much needed supplies for them.

Slocum had to grin when he saw how Sarah June had expanded the Tons o' Gold Saloon. When he had left for Denver to give Simmons the note from his daughter, there had been only a single tattered tent at the edge of town. Now there were two and both were filled in spite of it being an hour until sundown.

He knew he ought to press on and find Rebecca to let her know about her father's peculiar reaction, but facing the fiery redhead was less important to him at the moment than ducking into the Tons o' Gold and talking to Sarah June again. Slocum tied his horse to a post outside the new tent and poked his head inside. This tent was set up as a gambling hall. A faro game ran just inside the door and four battered tables had been set up for poker or blackjack near the rear. A small slit in the tent allowed a waiter to bring in drinks from the other, larger tent with its bar.

"You up for a game, mister?" called a scruffy-looking man dressed in a long cutaway coat that had seen better days. He riffled through a deck of cards with an expertise that told Slocum the professional gamblers had discovered Bonanza.

"Later," Slocum said, wondering if the gambler was legit or if he was one of the breed who thought he could make more money cheating. If the latter, Slocum would gladly run him out of Sarah June's establishment. After all, Sarah June had told him he could run the gambling in the Tons o' Gold. Even if he had abandoned that job only a day after the saloon had opened to go off on a wild goose chase delivering a letter for Rebecca.

"Go wet your whistle," the gambler said. "Best rotgut in Bonanza. And then mosey on back for a friendly game of stud poker. The cards'll call your name after a drink or two. Trust me." He expertly shuffled the cards and spread them in a fan in front of him on the table.

Slocum pushed aside the tattered edge of the slit in the tent and went into the main saloon. Abel worked diligently at cleaning the hodgepodge of glasses they used for their patrons. At least this had not changed. Slocum should have ordered real shot glasses from a supplier in Denver but had not thought of it when he was there. Besides, the shipment would have come through the canyon controlled by Malcolm Newcombe and probably would not have arrived intact. He could not imagine bringing glassware into Bonanza going down into Knife Canyon and then back up the sheer face of rock.

"Hey, Mr. Slocum. Good to see you again. Drink?"

"Why not?" Slocum said, leaning against the bar. It had lost a nail or two since he'd put it together and creaked under his weight. "Where's Sarah June?"

"Miss Daniels is out and about, prob'ly jawin' with them two miner friends of hers. Said she'd be back by the time the crowd showed up for their evening prayer meetin'. I do declare, some of those miners really do worship demon rum."

Slocum looked around at the bustle in the tent.

"This isn't the crowd?"

"No, sir, it sure ain't. We get so many in here they can't even fall over when they pass out. When Miss Daniels added that there tent for the gamblin', things really picked up steam."

"Glad to hear it."

He sipped at the whiskey and made a face. It was trade whiskey.

"Sorry, Mr. Slocum. That there's the best we got right now. Did I put in too much gunpowder?"

"Too much nitric acid," Slocum said. His tongue burned from the potent concoction.

"Can't get it right. I'm always puttin' too much or not enough or something." Abel frowned and shook his head sadly. "Miss Daniels gave me the recipe but I don't read so good and have to try remembering the formula."

"Don't worry, Abel. Business is booming." Slocum cringed when a distant explosion shook the ground.

"That's been goin' on ever since a supply train of gunpowder and other diggin' tools came in yesterday."

Slocum watched the miners in the saloon and saw that Sarah June had been right. The real mother lode was selling whiskey, not grubbing out silver from a reluctant vein of sulfite meandering through a hard rock mountain.

"I've got some business to finish up and then I'll be back to talk with Sarah June."

"I'll let her know if she gets back 'fore you do, Mr. Slocum."

Slocum downed the rest of the poisonous whiskey, let it puddle and burn in his belly for a moment, then left. The sun was sinking behind the high mountains, casting long shadows and producing the usual, razor-edge wind that kicked up at twilight. Shivering, he pulled his coat around him a little tighter and set off down the street, heading for the Eldorado Hotel. The sooner he told Rebecca Simmons what had happened in Denver, the sooner he could wash his hands of the whole affair. It never paid to get pulled in two directions at the same time, and he ought to have known better than to leave Sarah June to run the saloon just to deliver a letter.

Making a few dollars gambling in the Tons o' Gold before moving on looked better and better.

Slocum slowed and then stopped in front of the bakery when he spotted Rebecca, her coppery hair gleaming like gold in the setting sun, talking with Buster Newcombe. It took Slocum only an instant to realize they weren't merely talking. The two stood nose to nose and argued heatedly. He caught snippets of what they said, but the rising wind muffled the words and not the tone.

Rebecca finally drove her index finger into Newcombe's chest and pushed him back. She took a step after him and poked him again. Then he angrily batted her hand away and stormed off. The woman started after him, fists clenched in fury, then subsided. She stamped her foot in pique, whirled, and stormed into the hotel.

Slocum was slow to follow so she wouldn't think he had been spying on her, and reached the hotel lobby as Rebecca started up the stairs to her room on the second floor.

"Miss Simmons!" he called.

"Mr. Slocum. You're back!" She looked up the stairs, as if considering where they should discuss his trip. She came back down the steps and indicated the small, shabby parlor to the side of the lobby. Her hair was in disarray, as much from the wind as her argument, and her pale cheeks were flushed. Slocum could not tell if it was from the cold wind whipping down Bonanza's main street or the fervor of her argument with Newcombe.

He sat in a chair and looked back into the lobby. The clerk eyed him with open jealousy. Rebecca Simmons was a lovely woman, and anyone talking to her was likely to get such a response from the homely clerk. Slocum ignored him and turned his attention to Rebecca. She perched on the edge of the chair, hands folded in her lap and looking as if she was taking tea at some society soirée.

"I did not expect you back so quickly, John," she said. "Did you use Newcombe's toll road?"

"I went through Markam Pass," he said. Her eyes widened slightly. Excitement built in her at these words.

"Then you saw firsthand how a rail could be laid through there! Splendid! Did you tell this to my father?"

"I saw him on his train in Denver. He had me thrown off."

"Oh, pish. He can be difficult, but my letter would have introduced you properly. What did he say?"

"He said that the letter was a forgery and you never did know what you were talking about. He said he had no interest in putting a spur into Bonanza from Kennicut."

"He's always skeptical of new projects. Ask anyone."

"Like the three thugs he told to throw me off his train?"

"You didn't let them, did you?" she asked hesitantly. Then Rebecca's opinion firmed. "No, you would never let them do a thing like that. What did my father say about a starting date? We need surveyors to begin work right away, of course."

"He wasn't interested." Slocum wasn't sure what it would take to convince the redhead he was not embellishing what had happened when he had seen Colonel Simmons.

"You *did* speak to my father?"

"If he rides in a train with a fancy coffin in the last car," he said. At mention of the coffin, Rebecca recoiled as if he had struck her in the head with an ax handle. "Whose coffin is that? It looked as if he had lain down inside it, but he seemed hale and hearty."

"It's his," she said reluctantly. "He never goes anywhere without it. It . . . it is a little eccentricity of his. Quite harmless, though. But you did not find when he intended bringing in a crew to build the bridge across Knife Canyon?"

Slocum felt as if he were pissing into the wind. The only thing he could do was stop.

"I told you what he said. He didn't believe me or accept your letter."

"Why didn't you make him?" she asked, irritation mounting now.

Slocum was not going to argue the point. Colonel Simmons had not given him the opportunity, and in this regard his daughter was much the same. They both heard what they wanted and expected the world to fall into place.

"I've got to go," Slocum said, standing.

"But you must take another letter to him. If what you say is true, the CGRR will be left out of a wonderful venture. We can help the fine people of Bonanza and get rich at the same time. Everyone prospers if the railroad comes to town soon."

"Except Malcolm Newcombe and his son," Slocum said, tossing this out to watch Rebecca's reaction. Her jaw tensed, and she ground her teeth. Color rose in her cheeks.

"What do I care if they are ruined? A toll road! Imagine such a plebeian venture!"

"I wish you luck convincing your father to build the railroad across Knife Canyon. Maybe if you saw him in person, you could convince him. But I doubt it."

"Why, I never—" Rebecca sputtered at such impertinence. Slocum tipped his hat to her and left, angling across the lobby. He saw the broad smile on the clerk's face, as if he considered Slocum out of the running in the quest for Rebecca Simmons's heart.

Slocum stepped into the cold wind whipping along Bonanza's only street and saw how Sarah June had started bonfires at two corners of the Tons o' Gold to draw patrons. Not only did it make her saloon stand out, it afforded the miners a place to warm their hands before they entered to warm their bellies with Abel's fierce tarantula juice.

Head down against the wind, Slocum went to the saloon and slipped into the main tent. Abel had been right. The crowd before now seemed small. Miners now pressed in, shoulder to shoulder. Lilting laughter drew him through the crush to where Sarah June sat, joking and enticing the miners to buy drinks.

"John!" she cried, jumping up and making a path through the crowd to get to him. "You came back!"

"You sound surprised," he said.

"I . . . I'm not," she said, obviously lying. Sarah June had thought he would vanish into the hills and never be seen again. "Did you finish your business?"

"It's done, but it wasn't successful," he said. "Enough of that. I see business is booming."

Sarah June laughed over the tumult in the tent. "You can say that." She edged closer and said so only he could hear, "Maybe later on we can make something else boom."

This took him aback. He started to ask if, contrary to what she had said before, she had decided to mix business and pleasure, but the demands of the miners swept her away. She waved to Abel, got his attention, and two waiters brought stacks of glasses and two bottles of the pitiful whiskey conjured up behind the saloon.

Slocum let himself be carried off by the crowd and ended up in the gambling tent, where he found himself in a game of five card draw. He walked away with more than twenty dollars by the time he found himself in need of fresh air. The constant press of miners wore him down. He was used to wide-open spaces, not jam-packed rooms.

He stepped into the crisp Colorado night and took a deep, refreshing breath. In spite of his intolerance for so many bodies pressed so close together, he felt as if he belonged here. Looking forward to finding out what Sarah June had meant about getting together after closing set his heart pounding a bit faster, too.

As he stood by one of the raging bonfires at the edge of the saloon tent, he stared down Bonanza's main street and wondered at the half-dozen horses tethered in front of the hotel. The single gunshot from the Eldorado focused his attention on the men running from the hotel and hastily getting onto their horses.

A smaller figure in the grip of one man struggled and fought to get free.

"Rebecca!" he shouted, going for his six-shooter. Slocum took off at a run, covering the distance to the hotel faster than a racehorse. As he got closer he saw how Roy

Eachin held Rebecca firmly in front of him and how she struggled, trying to bite him or claw and kick her way free. He was too strong.

And Eachin held a smoking six-gun in his hand.

His horse wheeled about and Eachin fired twice at Slocum, stopping his headlong rush to rescue Rebecca.

Eachin kicked hard, and his horse rocketed off. The other five men pounded after him, leaving only fitful whirls of dust in the air to mark their retreat. In a few seconds, the strong wind had erased even this sign they had been in Bonanza.

Slocum dashed into the lobby and saw the clerk sprawled over the counter. A six-shooter lay on the floor where it had slipped from lifeless fingers. The clerk had tried to save Rebecca and had paid for it with his life.

Slocum saw nothing could be done here and ran back to the Tons o' Gold, where he had tied his horse. The tired mare protested the weight on her back after an evening of leisure. Slocum retraced his route and got on Eachin's trail fast. Slocum rode hard but Eachin had a head start and went directly to the mouth of the canyon where the toll road began. He, his men, and Rebecca Simmons were safe behind the barbed wire fence by the time Slocum thundered up.

Staring at the newly rebuilt blockhouse and the savage, barbed wire fence convinced Slocum of the folly of going after Eachin. No fewer than a half-dozen rifles poked over the top of the guardhouse, and in the trees on either side of the road drifted shadowy figures. He would go up against a dug-in, fortified army just itching to ventilate him if he tried to rescue the redheaded woman.

He had to get help against Newcombe and his henchman and he had to get it fast, for Rebecca's sake.

7

There was no marshal in Bonanza, and Slocum would not have wanted to go to any lawman in any case. Men like Malcolm Newcombe were rich enough to buy the law. Slocum rode back to town, wondering if he could get Abel to help him. Before he reached the Tons o' Gold Saloon, he had discarded that wild notion. There wasn't anyone in Bonanza he could trust. Abel was a fair teamster, a good bartender, and an honest man, but Slocum refused to risk his—and Rebecca's—life to someone who was hardly dry behind the ears. If shooting started, he had to rely on anyone with him and not worry how they might get themselves shot up out of inexperience.

Slocum entered the noisy, crowded saloon tent and looked around. His spirits sank. The miners wanted nothing but to get drunk and forget about their failure to strike it rich. They had not toiled long enough yet to become discouraged and open to riding with Slocum on what might be a suicide mission.

"You gonna stand there or you gonna let me in to get a drink?"

61

Slocum turned to see a huge man in buckskins behind him.

"I'll buy you a drink if you'll deliver a message to Kennicut for me." The words slid from Slocum's lips before he thought.

The man snorted and shook his shaggy head. "That's a killer of a trip. I crossed Knife Canyon twice in the last month. No reason for me to do that again any time soon."

"You're not a miner," Slocum said, sizing the mountain man up fast. "You have the look of a hunter about you."

"And you look like a shootist," the huge man said amiably. "I don't want to tangle with you, but will if you don't move so I can get my liquor. It's mighty dry up there in the hills."

"I'll buy you the drink and give you twenty dollars to get to Kennicut as fast as you can and send a telegram."

"That's mighty generous, mister, but I been tricked so many times I can't count 'em." The man's eyes widened when he saw the roll of greenbacks Slocum pulled from his pocket. Slocum peeled off twenty dollars and handed it to the hunter.

For a moment, the huge man said nothing. Then, "How do you know I won't light out and rob you of your money?"

"Another fifty when you get back with a reply. I'll leave it with Abel there."

"You might be in cahoots," the hunter said, but Slocum saw he was coming around to accepting. This was more money than the man had seen in months, and all Slocum was asking of him was a simple, week-long trip. "What's this message you want delivered? It's got to be powerful important."

Slocum found a scrap of paper and a pencil and carefully printed what he wanted telegraphed to Colonel Simmons. From the way the man stared at it blankly, he could not read. That was fine with Slocum. It would make it more likely any delivered reply would actually come from Simmons.

"You must put a powerful lot of store in getting an answer," the hunter said. "What if your friend doesn't see fit to reply?"

"Wait a few days. If there isn't a telegram by the time you run through your twenty dollars, come on back. The rest of the money'll still be yours."

"You got a trusting heart, mister."

Slocum had no choice. He bought the hunter a second drink and got the man on the trail to Kennicut. With luck, Colonel Simmons would know that Newcombe had kidnapped his daughter in a few days. What his response would be, Slocum could not say.

With even more luck, Slocum would have Rebecca free by dawn.

Slocum rolled onto his belly to keep the bulge of ammunition in his coat pocket from distracting him. His six-shooter was loaded, but he wanted to rely on the Winchester for serious shooting, if it came to that. Slocum preferred to use his trusty knife to keep from drawing unwanted attention.

Wriggling to the fence, Slocum forced up the bottom strand of barbed wire and started to crawl under it when he heard a distant clinking sound. He cursed under his breath and slithered like a snake to get entirely under. The distant sound came from a stone in a tin can dangling from the wire—a crude alarm system.

Slocum dug his toes into the soft dirt and sprinted for a clump of bushes near a few stunted piñons. He dropped to his belly, aimed his rifle in the direction of the clinking sound, and waited. The guards might be asleep and would not have heard. Or they might ignore it.

Slocum cursed again when he saw two men with shotguns resting in the crooks of their arms slowly walking along the fence, looking at the bottom strand for any breaks. He was glad he had not cut the wire, but dealing with a pair of guards might prove too much. Any ruckus now would bring more guards down on his neck.

On impulse, Slocum threw back his head and let out a coyote howl. He waited a few seconds and repeated it. The guards spun, their scatter guns too-accurately pointing in his direction. Then his luck changed. A lovelorn coyote across the canyon returned the howl. The guards relaxed, laughed, and stopped their circuit, going back to the warmth of the blockhouse.

After a few minutes, Slocum left his hiding place and slipped deeper into the woods before angling toward the toll road. He reached the dirt track and looked deeper into the canyon, then back at the blockhouse. Eachin would not keep Rebecca there at the gate. It was too easy for anyone using the road to see the captive and ask questions. In spite of their overwhelming superiority, Newcombe's guards could not hope to succeed if enough travelers knew they were holding a woman against her wishes. This was the frontier with rough and ready justice, and Newcombe had made enough of the men in Bonanza angry charging both to enter and to leave the toll road.

More than this, a kidnapped woman might provide a rallying point for the miners to break the stranglehold Newcombe had on their supplies.

Another thought came to Slocum. He had not heard of the miners trying to get their silver out of Bonanza and back to Denver or other places where the precious metal could be exchanged for power, both financial and political. He didn't doubt for an instant much of the silver would never arrive if shipped along the toll road, making Newcombe even richer and the miners even madder.

He had arguments to rally the miners, but that would take time. Slocum wasn't sure the lovely redhead had time. Eachin had failed with Sarah June. He wasn't likely to make the same mistake twice.

Turning into the inky darkness of the canyon, Slocum began walking fast. He covered a considerable amount of ground before sunrise and never caught sight of any spot where Eachin might be holding Rebecca. For two days he hunted for the kidnapped woman, to no avail. Heartsick at his failure and what it meant for Rebecca's safety, he finally returned to Bonanza.

"You just up and vanish all the time, Mr. Slocum?" asked Abel. "It surely did bother Miss Daniels. She moped around for a couple days. Wasn't 'til last night she perked up. Might have been them two miner friends of hers, but I think it was jist gettin' over not seein' you that lifted her spirits."

Slocum sloshed the potent liquor around in the jelly jar Abel had filled for him. Drinking on an empty stomach was not too smart, and he had not taken much time to hunt for game in the canyon while hunting for Rebecca Simmons. The truth was, Slocum had felt more like the hunted. He had been surrounded by patrolling armed guards and risked discovery at any instant. If he had been found, Rebecca would have been doomed.

Who else was there to save her?

"You live here?" came a deep-throated growl Slocum recognized at once. He spun around and saw the hunter he had sent with the message to Colonel Simmons. "Or you just waitin' for me?"

"You couldn't have made it to Kennicut and back this fast."

"I used my brains," the hunter said, tapping the side of his shaggy head. "There's a couple kids with mirrors.

They send messages back and forth across Knife Canyon all the time. I got them to handle the message." The hunter took a drink from Abel and downed it in a single mighty gulp. He belched. "Good thing they got more 'n a smidgen of schoolin'."

"The telegram was sent?"

"Got a reply, too. The little kid, name of Patrick, copied this down for me." The hunter passed a yellowed sheet of paper to Slocum, who quickly scanned it.

Slocum went cold inside. It was as he had feared.

"Not good news, is it?" the hunter asked. "That's what both Patrick and his friend thought."

"Colonel Simmons won't send any help to rescue his daughter."

"Rescue? Them Utes on the warpath? Or is it the Arapahos? They're nasty ones."

"It's Malcolm Newcombe and his henchman who kidnapped her."

"Colonel Simmons is a real important fellow, isn't he?" asked the hunter. "Puts in railroads?"

"He's the one. His daughter was here to decide if they should build a bridge over Knife Canyon and bring the railroad to Bonanza."

"That'd make life in Bonanza a sight easier," the hunter said, "but it would put Patrick and his friend out of business."

Slocum laughed at this. Then he sobered. Rebecca remained in Eachin's clutches, and the only significant help she could have expected had been denied. He had to wonder if Colonel Simmons was really her father from the way he acted.

"You got the rest of my money?"

"Here it is," Slocum said, peeling off fifty in greenbacks from the wad in his pocket. He had a lot less now than before sending the hunter out on a futile mission, but he had tried.

Now he would have to try harder—or think of a new way to find Rebecca.

"Money," Slocum said, more to himself than to either Abel or the hunter. "You earn money."

"You've been gamblin' for it, Mr. Slocum," said Abel. "At least, that's what Miss Daniels expects from you."

"You earn it with a job." He took a deep breath and left the saloon. What he intended doing was about the stupidest thing he had ever done, but he couldn't let Rebecca stay in Eachin's—and Newcombe's—grip.

He turned his back on the Tons o' Gold Saloon with some regret and rode out of Bonanza, heading down the steep trail that led to the mouth of the canyon. This time he approached boldly, although he was keyed up. He banked on Eachin being occupied with his captive. And Slocum doubted Buster Newcombe spent any time with the guards. Those were the only two likely to identify him, although one or two of the guards might. The only time he had been seen by the men at this end of the toll road was when Jessup had bulled his way through.

The scent of the burned blockhouse still hung in the air. None of the guards would have singled Slocum out when their miniature fort was burning down around their ears.

"Howdy, mister," called a sturdy man who sauntered over from where he had been drinking coffee with two other guards. "You ready to leave Bonanza behind and all its silver?"

"I'm looking for a job," Slocum said. "Anything beats scrabbling around in the dirt for a few ounces of silver."

"Well, now, why don't you just come on in so we can talk this over. Might be Mr. Newcombe can use a new guard." The man eyed Slocum critically, seeing the well-worn ebony handle of the Colt Navy on his left hip and they way Slocum moved. He had to like what he saw or he would have turned Slocum away.

The gate creaked open and Slocum rode through, knowing how foolhardy this was and how little choice he had if he wanted to find Rebecca Simmons.

8

It galled Slocum to stand by as Newcombe's men fleeced the teamsters and miners on their way through the canyon. But he stood with his rifle in hand, watching alertly and wondering where Eachin had taken Rebecca. All day long he made certain the travelers paid until it was mid-afternoon and the other guards were getting sleepy.

"Siesta time," said Murdoch, the guard who had hired Slocum. "Me and the other boys want to get some sleep. Bein' newest, you're the one to watch the fence."

"Got it," Slocum said to Murdoch. He waited anxiously for the guards to find places under trees or in the warm sun to go to sleep. He was sure Eachin and his boss wouldn't like the way the guards curled up to snooze like lizards on a hot rock, but the sentry on the far canyon rim had not sent any mirror messages letting them know another wagon train was on its way through. This meant nothing but boredom lay ahead for the next few hours.

This suited Slocum just fine.

Murdoch nodded, gave Slocum a once over as if trying to place him, then shrugged it off. Slocum didn't know if Murdoch had seen him when Jessup's wagons had fought their way through to Bonanza, but it was possible. Not knowing how good Murdoch's memory was, Slocum kept his face averted as much as possible while trying to look alert.

The guards were soon snoring peacefully, and Slocum had his chance to explore. He rode the fence for a ways until he was out of sight of the blockhouse, then cut back to the road through the canyon. He had searched the entire area on foot for the better part of two days and had found nothing. This time he was going to try a different tack.

Instead of following the road, he cut through the forest on the other side of the road. He made better time now, being mounted, and spotted what he had missed before. A small curlicue of smoke rose some distance away from the road. Riding in the woods proved more difficult than he had anticipated, but Slocum stuck with it. Soon, the scent of burning piñon made his nose wrinkle. Along with the wood smoke came the fragrance of cooking food.

By accident Slocum crossed a narrow path. He reined back and knew he was close now. Taking the path away from the main road, he soon found a small clearing. Slocum's heart jumped into his throat when he saw a cabin and a trio of horses tethered behind it. The smoke he had seen earlier came from the stone chimney.

"Three horses," Slocum mused. Three guards? Including Eachin? He dared not make a mistake now. If Eachin saw him, the gunfight would begin.

Dismounting, Slocum advanced on foot. The three horses whinnied in protest at a stranger approaching, but Slocum took it slow and easy and the horses soon subsided. He looked for a way to peer into the cabin, but unlike the blockhouses, this was well-constructed. Slocum whipped out his knife and carefully worked the dried mud from between logs until he had his peephole.

He saw dim figures moving around but heard nothing.

Worse, he couldn't find Rebecca. She might be tied in a
far corner, blocked from his sight—or she might not be
in the cabin.

"I've got to go," came the muffled words. "My pa
wants to talk to me."

"Sure, Buster, go ahead," came the mocking answer.
"You go running off to your pa."

"Look, Eachin, you're one arrogant bastard and I won't
have you talking to me like that. You take orders from
me, not the other way around."

"Who would your pa keep around, if he had to choose
one of us?" demanded Eachin. The gunman moved into
Slocum's view. This might be the big blowout. Eachin
put his hand on his six-gun, as if he was ready to draw
down on the younger Newcombe. For his part, Buster
Newcombe squarely faced Eachin and did not back down.

"You think you could explain it to my father how you
shot me down?" Buster said. "Keep that hogleg of yours
where it belongs. And if you touch one hair on her head,
I'll see you in hell!"

"You just might," Eachin grumbled, but the henchman
backed down.

Slocum pulled away as the peephole suddenly went
dark when Buster Newcombe came toward him. He
thought he had been seen, then realized he had poked
through the wall next to where Rebecca was tied up.

"You'll be safe while I'm gone," Buster said to the
woman. "Eachin won't dare do anything to you, and if he
does, he answers to me!"

Those were brave words and ones Rebecca did not believe. Slocum heard her angry, muffled words. A gag kept
them from being completely understandable, but he got
the jist—she thought as poorly of Buster as she did of
Eachin.

Slocum lost sight of Buster Newcombe, but heard the

cabin door slam. He hurriedly ducked around the cabin in time to keep from being seen as the young man mounted and rode off. That left two in the cabin with Rebecca.

"Eachin," Slocum said, finding that he anticipated meeting the man face-to-face. He had told his stooge to throw Slocum over a cliff. That was a score that had to be evened.

But first Slocum had to be sure Rebecca was safe. Even as that determination came to him, he lost control of the situation. The second man had left the cabin at the same time as Buster Newcombe, but he had lingered before coming around. He spotted Slocum, and his eyes went wide in surprise.

It was the man who had been told to throw Slocum over the cliff.

"You!" the man cried as he fumbled to get out his six-shooter. If he had not revealed himself, he might have had a chance of shooting Slocum in the back. Slocum went into a gunfighter's crouch, drew, and fired before the man had cleared leather.

"You've got your clothes on," Slocum said, seeing that his bullet had flown straight and true through the man's heart. "They can bury you in them."

He knew the gunshot would spook Eachin. The man wasn't likely to come rushing out, but would hole up until he knew what he faced. The way the blockhouses had been built showed Newcombe and probably Eachin preferred defensive positions to offensive. Slocum stepped back and saw the roof overhang. He holstered his six-gun, jumped and caught at the eaves, kicked hard, and got enough momentum to pull himself up onto the steeply sloping roof.

He didn't hear Eachin come running out; he had figured the man would stay inside where he could use Rebecca as a shield. Slocum carefully walked across the roof, trying to make as little noise as possible. He found a patch of shake shingles that had started coming loose. Working steadily, Slocum pulled them off and left only a thin covering of tarpaper beneath.

He stood straight, drew his gun and stepped forward onto the paper. He plummeted downward and hit the cabin floor hard. Slocum let the power of the fall compress him into a tight crouch as he brought up his six-shooter.

Eachin stared in shock at the sudden entry. The man sputtered and swung his rifle around. Slocum fired an instant before Eachin, but knew instantly he had only winged the man. Eachin's slug went into the wall over Slocum's head—and Eachin stumbled out the front door.

"Ummm, ummm!"

Slocum glanced to his right and saw Rebecca struggling against her bonds. The gag kept her from making more than the muffled pleas for help as she kicked at the wall.

"I'll be back. I can't let that snake slither off. He's too dangerous." Slocum went to the door, chanced a quick glance around the jamb, then blasted outside when he did not spot Eachin.

The sound of a horse galloping off made Slocum curse. He should have hobbled the horses or just let them go free. He had left Eachin the perfect escape route. Slocum ran to the rear of the cabin in time to see Eachin bending forward over his horse's neck and racing into the woods surrounding the small clearing. Eachin would ride for cover, then swing around to reach the toll road to alert the guards.

Slocum knew he didn't have much time. He went back into the cabin and faced a furious Rebecca Simmons. She strained until her face almost matched the color of her fiery mop of red hair. Slocum slashed expertly with his keen-edged knife and freed her hands. She ripped the gag from her mouth.

"You left me in their clutches forever!" she raged.

"It took me a few days to find you," he said.

"Why? This is Buster's cabin. You could have come straight here. You should have known that fool wouldn't go anywhere else."

"Come on," Slocum said, ignoring her tirade. "Eachin got away. It won't be long until he fetches a small army to come for us."

"What? You let that son of a bitch get away!" Rebecca spun around and threw her arms up in the air in exasperation. "What kind of rescue is this?"

"One that's going nowhere unless you stop caterwauling and start cooperating," Slocum said harshly. His tone threw cold water on the woman's anger. She started to retort, then clamped her mouth firmly shut.

"There's a horse behind the cabin. Get it and I'll fetch my mare. You might want to take the six-shooter from the dead man."

"Dead man? Buster? You killed Buster?"

"The one who left with him. Newcombe rode off before he could have known of any trouble. It's Eachin we have to worry about."

Slocum frowned. He wasn't sure but it looked as if a flood of relief washed over the woman. That made no sense to him. Buster Newcombe was as responsible for kidnapping her as Eachin. In fact, he must have ordered his henchman to take her prisoner if Rebecca had been held captive in his cabin.

Slocum knew he should worry about the contradictions later. He ran to where he had left his mare, swung into the saddle and rode back as Rebecca clumsily mounted the horse. Her flouncy skirts got in the way, but she gamely ripped at them so she could ride astride.

"That way," Slocum said, pointing in the direction Eachin had ridden.

"But the road's in the other direction," she said.

"Do you think Eachin or Newcombe will ever let us simply ride out? We have to find another way out of here." Slocum looked upward toward the canyon rim, hundreds of feet above them. A sentry with a mirror—or possibly several men—was positioned there. He hoped this meant they had blazed a passable trail up the face of the canyon wall to relieve the men on the rim from time to time.

If there wasn't such a trail within the boundaries of the barbed wire fences at either end of the canyon, Slocum saw no way for him and Rebecca to ever escape.

"You certainly made a botch of freeing me," Rebecca said acidly as she trotted alongside Slocum.

"You're welcome," Slocum said sarcastically. "Especially since your father refused to help. I sent a telegram to him, and he wouldn't do anything."

Rebecca heaved a deep sigh and shook her head. "You don't understand," she said in a pensive tone. "The colonel isn't like other men."

"You're right. Other men would move heaven and earth to save their daughter," Slocum said.

"He has so much on his mind," she said. Rebecca turned slightly. The light slanting over the canyon rim caught her hair and turned it to coppery fire. Her pale skin was still flushed, and she looked like an angel with a glowing halo. "I have behaved poorly. Thank you, John. You didn't have to come after me and you did."

"I had to," he said. "I couldn't let Eachin kidnap you, and there's no law in Bonanza."

"Not much in Kennicut, for all that," she said. "There must be a sheriff somewhere, but I don't even know what the county seat is."

"I'm surprised," Slocum said. "I thought you knew everything."

"Why, you—" She sputtered and then checked her flare of anger. "I suppose I deserved that."

"You did," Slocum said. The words hung like lead until he and Rebecca reached the canyon wall. Then their attention turned to escape rather than bickering.

"Do you see any way up?" Rebecca asked.

"Not here, but there must be some way to reach the rim. This is the side where the sentries signal that a wagon train is coming along the toll road."

Slocum knew that to their left lay the gate leading to Bonanza. It was closer, and he saw no reason to scout a trail near it. More likely, the path to the top lay closer to the other gate. Walking his horse, picking his way through the tangle of thorny shrubs and low-growing bushes proved difficult, but Slocum was loath to head back toward the toll road. Pressing on as fast as they could was their only chance for staying alive, and that meant no backtracking.

"John, there. Look! Up high on the cliff!"

Rebecca had spotted the sentry before he had. The guard was not signaling but was only cleaning his mirror. The random flashes told Slocum the alarm had not gone out for them yet or the man would have been more cautious.

"Look at the rock face," Slocum said. His sharp eyes picked out the faint trail zigzagging back and forth. It was hardly more than a ledge, but it led to the rim. Getting up the path without being spotted was their next problem.

"We'll have to walk the horses," Rebecca said, seeing how narrow the path was. "I'm not sure I'm up for hiking that far."

"Then you'd better consider what it will be like when Eachin catches you again," Slocum said, dismounting. He took a few minutes to reload his six-shooter, then started up the faint trail. She sat on her horse, watching him in stony silence. But when he started up the steep path, she slid from the saddle and hurried to join him.

Slocum realized Rebecca was not much for apologizing, but she could be reasoned with. It only took a little doing, and he had to make it seem as if she was the one doing the choosing.

Halfway up, Slocum took a rest. Rebecca sank to a rock and panted harshly.

"The altitude," she explained. As she fanned herself, Slocum studied the canyon floor for any sign of pursuit. A half-dozen pilgrims made their way along the toll road, but nowhere did he spot Eachin or any sign of an organized hunt.

He took a deep drink from his canteen, then saw that Rebecca had none. He handed it to her and said, "Sorry. I didn't realize you didn't have any water."

Her green eyes fixed on him as she took the canteen and drank greedily. By force of will she stopped, corked the canteen, and handed it back.

"Thank you." She stared at him and finally said. "I've never met anyone quite like you, John. You're such a gentleman."

"That's the way I was raised," he said.

"Southern gentleman," she mused. "Not such a bad way to live."

"You make it sound foreign. Do all the men you know treat you the way your father does?"

"Why, no, well, yes, they do," she reluctantly admitted. "Business is so important. A moment's inattention to details and fortunes can be lost."

"A moment's inattention and a daughter can be lost," Slocum replied. He tugged on his mare's reins, got the unwilling horse moving, and continued up the path. As he crested the top of the trail, Slocum was ready for about anything.

He did not let down his guard when he saw they were alone on the ridge.

"Where is the man with the signal mirror?" Rebecca asked.

"I don't know, and I don't care," Slocum said. This meant one less man to kill. He had no quarrel with the sentry, other than working for someone like Malcolm Newcombe and Eachin. Under different circumstances, Slocum might have accepted a job with Newcombe as a guard and not thought twice about carrying out his duty for the toll road owner.

"What do we do?"

"Head for Bonanza," Slocum said, pointing along the canyon rim toward the boomtown. "There has to be a way off the ridge and into town." He did not know of one but had never sought it, either. All his exploration had been to the north, toward Markam Pass and the deep ravine separating Bonanza from Kennicut. "Do you remember anything of a map?"

"Not of this region," Rebecca said. "All I was interested in was building a bridge across Knife Canyon."

Slocum mounted and they started riding, warily watching for any hint that Newcombe's men had spotted them. From the canyon rim, Slocum had a decent view of everything happening below. The knot of travelers had left the Bonanza gate and a half dozen more wagons made their way down Newcombe's toll road. But he couldn't find any evidence Eachin was on their trail.

Slocum knew he had only winged the man. It had not been a serious enough a wound to kill him. If he had learned anything about men, Slocum knew the bullet hole in Eachin's worthless hide would only make him madder

and more determined than ever to recapture Rebecca—
and put Slocum six feet under.

"Down there," Rebecca said. "At the gate. Does it look
like more guards than usual?"

Slocum shielded his eyes against the setting sun and
studied the gate. Rebecca was right. A dozen guards
searched a wagon leaving the canyon. Eachin must have
thought Slocum and Rebecca had hidden in a wagon and
were trying to escape that way. If true, Slocum knew they
had successfully gotten away from Eachin. There was no
way he could send a posse of armed men up that narrow
trail after them before he and Rebecca reached Bonanza.
And with the sun setting, mirrors were going to be useless
for communicating in another few minutes.

"I'm getting cold, John," Rebecca complained. She
shivered as the cold wind whipped over the mountain
slopes.

"We'd better find a place to hole up for the night," he
said. His horse was beginning to stumble from exhaustion,
and as much as he wanted to get back to town, taking
care of the mare was of paramount importance now.

"Do we have to?" she asked. "I need to get to Kennicut
so I can contact my father."

"It's getting dark," Slocum said.

"I *have* to reach the colonel," she said. "Please, John.
We can keep going. Let's get back to Bonanza and rest
then."

Slocum started to argue, then decided not to. Handling
Rebecca required all the skill of a master powder monkey
using fulminate of mercury. He nodded briskly and let his
mare set her own pace through the gathering darkness.

Only when they reached the point of being completely
unable to see did Rebecca finally agree to stop for the
night. By then, Slocum wasn't sure if it was a good thing
or not.

9

"It's so cold, John," Rebecca Simmons said from beside him, shivering hard. She moved a little closer. "The wind's died down but the ground is cold."

Rebecca might have been right about the temperature of the ground, but she was mighty warm. Slocum felt her slipping closer. Somehow, the red-haired beauty's blanket lifted and then dropped so she could press against him. He felt her breasts crushing into his side as she snuggled even closer. Then he grew hot when her hand moved across his chest and slid lower over his belly. She squeezed gently until he began to stiffen with desire.

Slocum had wanted to avoid this. He was drawn to the lovely woman, but a wariness filled him whenever he thought about Rebecca—and the way her father treated her. They were different from any folks he had known, and he couldn't figure out why. Being rich was one thing, but it was as if they had been raised by wolves. Neither showed a great deal of affection for the other. That had to carry over to the way they dealt with other folks.

Including him.

Slocum sucked in his breath when he felt Rebecca's

clever fingers working open his fly, button by button. He couldn't help responding. His manhood snapped out, rigid and ready. Her slender fingers caught his length and began working up and down until he groaned a little from the sheer pleasure of it.

"I'm not hurting you, am I?" she asked, her breath hot against his cheek.

"Just the opposite," he said.

"Good." She nibbled at his ear, kissed at it, and then lightly nipped. The entire time her mouth was working on his ear and cheek and lips, her hand maintained its steady up-and-down motion on his fleshy staff.

Slocum's arms circled the woman's trim body and pulled her even closer. He returned her kisses with growing fervor as he felt the sexual need mounting within him. Mixing business and pleasure was wrong. He had heard that somewhere recently. The source flitted about like an annoying bug until he remembered who had said it.

Sarah June Daniels.

They were partners in an odd way. The Tons o' Gold Saloon was entirely Sarah June's, but she had given him the lucrative gambling concession. He had ignored taking advantage of the golden opportunity and was not sure why. Rebecca Simmons was a seductive woman, rich and lovely, smart and powerful, but he had resisted greater temptations in the past. Why had he thrown in with her, doing her bidding, rescuing her from Eachin and Newcombe while turning his back on Sarah June?

"Don't mix business and pleasure." Sarah June's words rang in his ears. He kissed Rebecca even harder, eliciting a moan that he ignored. It was not pain, it was pleasure. All pleasure and not business. He could never do business with the likes of Rebecca and her father.

Slocum began exploring on his own. She held him firmly, stroking insistently as he pushed his hand under

her skirts and found a warm inner thigh. He stroked over
the tender flesh as he worked his way ever upward. She
gasped with pure delight when he thrust his finger into
the tight recess hidden away between her legs.

"So nice, John," she cooed, "but I want something more
there. Something bigger. Something like *this*." She gave
him an unneeded tug to show him exactly what she
wanted.

Slocum rolled on top of her. The blanket that had covered them fluttered off in the light wind, making his back
cold. But the heat building in his loins more than offset
it. He pushed Rebecca's legs apart and hiked her skirts
even more as he positioned himself.

"There, John, yes, yes!" she cried as he levered his hips
forward. The blunt knob on the end of his manhood parted
her soft nether lips. Slocum paused for a moment as intense heat from her center warmed him and hardened his
rod even more.

Only when he caught his breath did he slip forward
with agonizing slowness. She trembled and moaned as he
thrust into her. The woman's female sheath was moist and
clinging all around him. The tightness made him want to
thrust fast and hard, but he took his time and teased her
with the promise of even more to come.

Rebecca lifted her rump off the ground and began ro-
tating her hips, grinding her hips in an attempt to get even
more of Slocum's hot, fleshy sword into her sheath.

"Do it, do it, oh, John, do it!" she shrieked.

He sank another inch down and stopped when he was
completely engulfed by her hot, hungry flesh. He felt rip-
ples inside as she tensed and relaxed around him. Slocum
thought he could stay awhile, but quickly realized that was
not going to be possible. She sucked his iron control
away, just as the wind pulled away his warmth.

Slocum drew back with a lewd sucking sound, then

slammed forward. His rapid reentry lifted her off the ground. She cried out and Slocum knew he was giving her what she wanted, what she needed. He began moving with quick, sure strokes that heated them both with the friction of his passage.

Feeling as if a powder keg had been buried in his balls, he moved faster and faster until the fuse was lit and there was no turning back. Hips flying, he fell into the age-old rhythm of a man loving a woman. Rebecca shuddered under him, then arched her back and ground her crotch into his. The lusty woman's movement all around him sapped his control and finally set him off.

The powder keg in his loins exploded.

As he arched his back in a vain attempt to sink even deeper into the wanton woman's core, Slocum heard her gasp and felt her shudder powerfully again. He spilled his seed and then sank down on top of her. Their faces were inches away, but Slocum felt as if they were a thousand miles apart. Whatever Rebecca had been thinking about still occupied her.

Slocum rolled to one side and let her snuggle closer. She buried her face in his chest where he felt the soft, even flow of her breath as the sexual thrill of their love-making faded.

"That was wonderful, John. But I knew it would be. Everything you do is so competent."

"Competent," he said, shaking his head. It was about what he expected from her, although he had hoped for more. Or had he? Slocum knew she had been thinking of someone else—and he had been thinking about Sarah June.

He laughed without humor. They had both made love and had been with someone else even as their bodies touched and melted together in lust.

Slocum lay on his back holding Rebecca close. Neither

said a word and soon enough, she drifted off to sleep. Slocum was slower to go back to sleep with his thoughts rolling over and over but never getting anywhere.

"What if they come for me again, John?" Rebecca asked. They had arrived in Bonanza before noon and had gone directly to the Eldorado Hotel. "I was afraid Eachin would be here waiting for me."

"You had better hightail it out of here," Slocum advised. "There's no marshal or sheriff to go to for protection. Even if there was, he'd probably be in Newcombe's hip pocket."

"I know that's the way it works in most places, but you don't know how far reaching my father's influence can be. The governor of Colorado is a close friend of his, as are the senators and all manner of local politicians."

"Elsewhere, but not in Bonanza. There's not even a mayor yet. Malcolm Newcombe controls access to town with an iron hand, so that makes him the power to deal with." Slocum heaved a deep sigh. "You'd better find someone to take you directly to Kennicut. It's a hard trip, but if you take it slow you can reach the town in a week."

"Very well," Rebecca said, heaving a deep sigh. "I feel as if I am giving up, but it really isn't like that. In Kennicut I can telegraph my father and convince him of the money to be made here. Bonanza is just that, a true bonanza! Why, getting a rail line into town is only a matter of crossing Knife Canyon."

"Only," Slocum said, remembering the sheer sides and the flash of vertigo he had experienced looking over the brink for the first time.

"Father will authorize it. He trusts my judgment in these matters," she said.

"He wouldn't even come to rescue you from Newcombe's clutches," Slocum pointed out.

"I explained that. He wants to instill a sense of inde-
pendence in me. And I don't want to run to him every
time I have a little problem."

Slocum didn't think of being kidnapped as a "little
problem." He started to ask Rebecca what Roy Eachin
and Buster Newcombe had done to her in the days before
he rescued her, but he held back. If she had wanted to
tell him, she would have. Rebecca was a strong-willed
woman and wasn't likely to do anything she did not intend doing.

Except getting kidnapped and maybe raped.

"If you leave in the morning, you can be in Kennicut
before you know it," Slocum said.

"You make it sound as if you won't be accompanying
me." Rebecca put a hurt tone into her voice. "How else
can I cross Knife Canyon?"

"You stay put for now here in the hotel. I don't want
you out where Eachin might grab you again."

"You're not coming up to . . . keep me company?" she
asked. Her green eyes boldly locked with his. Slocum felt
as if he was being given an order, and he did not like it
much.

"I'll look in on you later," he hedged. "After I take care
of other business."

"I'll be waiting," Rebecca said softly.

"Is she around?" Slocum asked Abel. The Tons o' Gold
Saloon was crammed full of miners all begging to get
drunk.

"You mean Miss Daniels?" The barkeep shook his
head. "Don't know where she is tonight. I reckoned she
would be in by now, but—" Abel shrugged eloquently,
showing his ignorance about his boss's whereabouts.

Slocum felt a little hollow inside, thinking Sarah June's
absence might mean she had found someone to distract

her from her thriving business. There had to be miners who had struck it rich and who were willing to lavish silver nuggets and endless attention on the pretty brunette. And Abel had mentioned before how she was keeping company with two miners.

"You want me to tell her you was in, Mr. Slocum?" asked Abel.

"I'll be back later," Slocum said, wondering if he would be. Rebecca had been clear in her intentions when she had invited him to her hotel room. He was a fool if he didn't take her up on it. Rebecca Simmons was lovely and rich and willing. So why was he feeling as reluctant as a cow starting down the chutes toward the slaughterhouse?

Slocum shrugged it off and stepped from the saloon tent into the chilly night. He sucked in a deep lungful of air and set off for the hotel. During the day four more wagons had come through Newcombe's toll road carrying equipment and another gaggle of puppy-dog eager miners. He had heard the buzz that no fewer than ten more wagons would follow in a day or two, bringing merchants and supplies.

He headed down the short street to the hotel, then reached for his six-shooter when he saw the horse tethered in front of the Eldorado. Slocum recognized Buster Newcombe's horse immediately. Looking around, Slocum made sure the rest of Newcombe's men were nowhere to be seen. He doubted Buster had come by himself, not with Eachin wounded and undoubtedly so angry he could chew nails and spit tacks at losing his hostage to Slocum.

Boots pounding in the dust, Slocum skidded to a halt in front of the hotel. He drew his six-gun and then slipped it back into the holster. Buster and Rebecca stood in the doorway, chest to chest, eye to eye.

"You leave me alone. If I so much as see one greasy hair on your head, I swear I'll cut it off—under your chin!" Rebecca stabbed out with her finger and moved Buster Newcombe back a half step.

Buster sputtered and then jerked away from the red-haired woman as if she had burned him with that finger. He stormed out of the hotel and jumped onto his horse. Slocum reached for his six-shooter again when he saw how cruelly Buster put his spurs to his horse's flanks. Then the younger man galloped out of sight.

Rebecca did not watch him ride off. She whirled angrily and flounced to the rickety stairs. Slocum heard every step creak under Rebecca's weight as she stomped her way to the second floor. A few seconds passed and then a distant door slammed hard enough to make the hotel shake. He scratched his head in wonder. Slocum knew he ought to follow Rebecca and ask what had gone on, but Rebecca would never give him a straight answer. Why she and Buster Newcombe had been together, why he had backed down and ridden away so fast, what was going on between them, was going to stay her secret.

Slocum decided Rebecca was safe enough for the night and headed for the stables, where he could bed down in the straw next to his horse. Somehow, this struck him as a better way of spending the night than with Rebecca.

It took only six days for Slocum and Rebecca Simmons to reach Kennicut, but it seemed longer since the entire way she was aloof. He had to admit he was not a fit trail companion, either, riding along thinking of Sarah June and how he had not seen her before leaving Bonanza. The arduous trail down and back up the walls of Knife Canyon took his mind away for a while, but he found himself wanting to head back to Bonanza.

He doubted Sarah June would cotton much to seeing him.

"Imagine," the redheaded woman said, looking around

Kennicut. "This town used to hold the promise Bonanza does now."

"It'll boom again, if only for a while, when building across the canyon begins," Slocum said.

Rebecca shrugged. "There's money to be made, but not here. In Bonanza."

She made it sound like a crusade now, a life's goal. Since she had argued with Buster Newcombe the night before leaving Bonanza, Rebecca had spoken more and more positively of putting a rail into the town. Slocum thought it might be as much a matter of putting the Newcombes out of business as it was of making money.

Slocum recoiled when a brass band launched into an off-key rendition of *Gary Owen*.

"What's that?" Rebecca said, irritated at having to shout over the loud music blaring throughout Kennicut.

"It's coming from the direction of the railroad depot," Slocum said. Without waiting to see if Rebecca followed, he rode toward the station. Every yard took him closer to the ear-shattering music played with more enthusiasm than skill.

Half the town gathered at the depot, all looking down the tracks with great anticipation.

"What's going on?" Slocum asked a citizen, shouting over the band.

"What? Oh, you're a stranger in these parts, aren't you?"

Slocum nodded rather than shouting his answer.

"Best durned thing what ever happened to Kennicut's rattlin' down the tracks. He ought to be here any time now."

"Who's that?"

"Why, only the smartest railroad man in the whole danged state of Colorado, that's who."

"General Palmer?" guessed Slocum, knowing the answer in spite of what he said.

The man laughed in delight and shook his head. "Nope. Colonel Simmons. We got word he's gonna build a trestle over Knife Canyon and put his narrow gauge into Bonanza. We're gonna get rich off supplying him workers."

Slocum looked in surprise at Rebecca. She smiled as if she had known all the time.

"I told you he always went with my suggestions," she said.

"But he wouldn't even—" Slocum bit off his denunciation of the woman's father. Simmons had rejected any rescue out of hand while going ahead with his plans to do what Rebecca had asked. It made no sense to him.

Just when Slocum thought the noise couldn't be any louder, a train whistle sounded and drowned out the brass band. In the distance, towering white plumes of steam gusted into the clear blue sky. A few seconds later the train rattled around a bend in the tracks and came into the Kennicut depot.

Slocum had seen the train before in Denver.

"Looks as if your pa's come to town," Slocum said to Rebecca. She never heard him. She stood in the stirrups and waved as frantically as any in the crowd, welcoming the owner of the Colorado Grand Mountain Railroad to town.

10

"That was a wonderful speech, Father. I've never heard you give a better one!" Rebecca exclaimed, grinning from ear to ear.

Slocum wondered if Colonel Simmons ever needed to breathe. The gaudily dressed popinjay had spoken for more than an hour, repeating himself often and never quite getting to the point. Slocum stood behind Rebecca as they crowded into the rear car in the train. Being in the same car as the fancy coffin made Slocum a tad uneasy, but not as uneasy as seeing Colonel Simmons again.

"Of course it was a great speech, my dear. I made it!" Simmons laughed as if he had told the best joke in the world. Gold medals on his chest bounced and flashed as he moved.

"You never mentioned that your daughter had been kidnapped," Slocum said.

"Who might you be, sir?" Colonel Simmons peered up at him, as if his memory was failing, but Slocum saw the recognition in the man's sharp eyes.

"John Slocum. You threw me off your train back in Denver a couple weeks ago."

"Since you are with my daughter, I assume . . ." Colonel Simmons let the words trail off, then laughed as if he had been told the lewdest joke in the world.

"That's right, Colonel," Slocum said before an embarrassed Rebecca could answer. "I'm the one who rescued her from Malcolm Newcombe."

"She never could do for herself," the railroad magnate said with some disdain. "Thank you for your fine work on her behalf, sir!" Colonel Simmons thrust out his hand. Slocum hesitated, then shook it. Hard.

The veins on his forearm popped out as he punished the owner of the Colorado Grand Mountain Railroad. The hand Slocum clutched had never held a hammer, never swung a military saber, never worked with anything more demanding than a pen poised over a checkbook. Colonel Simmons swallowed hard and blanched, but never let on how Slocum was crushing his hand mercilessly.

Slocum released his grip but felt no triumph over the man.

Simmons leaned against the coffin, then touched it lovingly. Slocum remembered what Rebecca had said about her father. Colonel Simmons was different from other men.

"Father, we need to discuss the trestle over Knife Canyon. We should begin work right away."

"Yes, you have been going on about a rail line into Bonanza. Why is it worth my effort to spend so much money getting there?"

Rebecca launched into her analysis of risk and reward. Slocum watched the colonel's eyes widen with avarice at the mention of how much silver poured from the Bonanza mines.

"Come along, my dear," Simmons said. "Let's discuss the matter at greater length in the parlor car." The two started forward on the train, deftly slipping past the coffin

that almost filled the car. Slocum wondered if such lithe-
ness came from simple agility or long practice at avoiding
the casket.

Then he wondered what he ought to do.

"John, come along," Rebecca said, pausing at the front
door. "Father will want to hear your appraisal of the situation in Bonanza." She made it sound as if she called a
dog.

Slocum slipped by the coffin, barely avoiding cutting
the mahogany with the hammer of his Colt Navy. He
twisted back and entered the posh rail car in front of the
one carrying the coffin. For a moment he was hesitant
about sitting. He was dirty from the trail and would leave
dusty marks if he sat. Then he figured it hardly mattered
to a man like Colonel Simmons. He had servants to clean
any filth he left behind.

"John can confirm this. Bonanza is, well, it is a bonanza! We can supply all equipment and most of the stock
for the general stores. This alone would guarantee a tre-
mendous return on the cost of getting the CGRR from
Kennicut to Bonanza."

Rebecca grabbed a sheet of paper from her father's
desk and began scribbling out her plans for the bridge
across Knife Canyon. Slocum sat quietly, wondering why
the hell he was even here. He started to get up and leave
when Rebecca said, "And John has been invaluable. Put
him on the payroll, Father."

"Fifty dollars a month?"

"A hundred," Rebecca said firmly, doing Slocum's bar-
gaining for him. "He will be worth it."

"Especially since I must see Bonanza for myself. You
will escort us, won't you, Mr. Slocum?"

"For a hundred a month, sure," Slocum said. "It'll take
about four days to get past Knife Canyon and through
Markam Pass to—"

"No!"

The sharpness of Colonel Simmons's reply startled Slocum.

"Why not?"

"I . . . I go nowhere without my belongings," Simmons said lamely.

Slocum glanced at Rebecca. She silently mouthed, "His coffin."

"You have to take the coffin?" Slocum said, astounded.

"Yes, it's necessary. One never knows what danger there is, and I need to know I can be buried properly should misfortune overtake me. Not in some horrible pine box or even in a blanket so the worms could eat my cold flesh." Simmons shuddered and turned even paler at the idea of being worm food after being buried in a mere saddle blanket.

Slocum had no sympathy for him. Too many of Slocum's partners over the years would have been buried in style if they had had even a blanket.

"What are you suggesting? We can't carry that box with us down the face of Knife Canyon. It's too steep." Slocum saw Rebecca's expression and almost walked away. "That's suicidal," he said flatly.

"But necessary, Mr. Slocum. Why are we paying you, if not to do my bidding?"

Rebecca interposed herself between Slocum and her father, whispering, "John, please. It won't be that bad."

"Eachin kidnapped you. Newcombe went along. There's no way they will let us use that toll road without killing us after what we've done to them. And there's no way to sneak through the canyon carrying that fancy burying box."

"We'll make it, John. You'll help us. Two hundred."

"What?"

"Two hundred a month, in advance."

Slocum couldn't be bought, but he could not allow Rebecca to waltz into Eachin's clutches again. It might mean his own death, but he had to be sure she didn't allow her crazy father to get her into a situation where she was in danger. He owed her that much.

"Yes, this is beautiful country. I love every inch of it," Colonel Simmons crowed as he rode along, staring up at the increasingly steep cliffs rising on either side of the canyon. "Rebecca, make a note to see who owns all this. It would make an excellent alternative to crossing Knife Canyon."

"Malcolm Newcombe owns it," Slocum said, "and it'll be a cold day in hell before he sells it to you. He's got the guns and the men and collects a fortune from everyone using his toll road. There's no reason for him to give it up just to please you."

"Every man has his price," Simmons said pompously.

Slocum did not reply. Simmons might be right, especially considering how he rode along with the railroad magnate and those in his entourage.

"There's the gate," Rebecca said, pointing it out to her father. Slocum studied her and saw how her pale cheeks glowed with red now. Her coppery hair was pulled back in a tight bun but some had escaped and gave her a wild, untamed look. Rebecca anticipated facing Eachin and Newcombe again and was excited by it.

Slocum wondered if it was Malcolm or Buster that put the most color in her cheeks.

"You!" bellowed a man from the farthest blockhouse.

Slocum's hand went for his six-shooter, but he did not draw. A half-dozen rifles aimed in their direction. He waited for Murdoch to bustle out and point an accusing finger at him.

"You lied to me. You didn't want a job. You shot Mr. Eachin!"

"How's he doing?" Slocum asked. "Poorly, I hope. For kidnapping Miss Simmons, he ought to be rotting in jail."

"We ain't lettin' you through. Go and—" Murdoch sputtered.

"My good man," Simmons said, riding over to the gate. His riding boots were so highly polished Slocum squinted as they reflected the early morning sun. Colonel Simmons wore his peculiar nonregulation uniform, replete with a half-dozen medals that Slocum couldn't recognize. Simmons was a poseur, but had an air of command about him that stopped Murdoch from raving on.

Slocum saw that Simmons's guards were getting ready for a fight. He wanted to tell them to stop preparing for a fight they could never win, but it had been clear from the day they had left Kennicut that the men were Simmons's and Simmons's alone. Even Rebecca had a difficult time getting them to do anything for her.

"We are willing to pay a premium to use Mr. Newcombe's fine toll road," Simmons said. "Would fifty dollars be enough?"

"Fifty? The toll is twice that for you and your wagon!"

"No, no," Simmons said. "That's fifty dollars for *you*, my good man. We will pay whatever the exact toll demanded by Mr. Newcombe, but the money is for your fine work in my behalf."

"What work?"

"Letting us through," Simmons said grandly.

Slocum couldn't believe that such a blatant bribe worked. Murdoch wasn't in a class with Eachin, but he was hardly lily pure, either. He opened the gate and came forward to talk quietly with Simmons. From the amount of money changing hands, Murdoch had held out for more than only fifty dollars. Maybe he would give it to the other guards to keep them quiet, maybe he intended to keep it all for himself. Slocum didn't know or much care. Colonel Simmons had money to burn.

"He is such a masterful man, isn't he?" Rebecca said to Slocum.

"That's one word for it," Slocum replied. He rode forward slowly, staying between Rebecca and the gunmen in the nearest blockhouse. The gate swinging shut behind Simmons's retinue would be no impediment to a quick retreat, but Slocum felt as if he had been sealed up in a high-security jail cell. They were completely at Newcombe's mercy now, armed guards ahead and behind and the sheer canyon walls on either side preventing any meaningful escape.

"Onward, lads!" cried Simmons, riding at the head of the column as if charging into battle. The wagon holding the colonel's coffin rattled and groaned as it began moving along the deeply rutted road. The other wagons with their supplies followed close behind.

Slocum rode to one side of the wagon train so he could talk to Rebecca.

"We'll be in Bonanza tomorrow," Rebecca said brightly. She looked around and tried not to appear to do so. Slocum wondered what she was searching for. Eachin? Buster Newcombe? He shared her need to locate them so he could keep them in plain sight. Having either of them behind him might mean taking a bullet to the back.

"If we keep up this pace, we can get out of the canyon by sundown," Slocum said. He wanted nothing more than to have Newcombe's toll road far behind him.

"My father might slow us so he can study the canyon. He's quite the geologist and engineer. The canyon is a better route for the railroad than across Knife Canyon."

Slocum snorted. Neither Simmons nor his daughter had listened to a word he had said. Malcolm Newcombe was getting rich from this toll road. No amount of money offered by the colonel would pry Newcombe loose from this goose laying one golden egg after another every time a wagon came through.

"Plan to go over Knife Canyon," Slocum advised. "How long would it take to build a trestle there?"

"Oh, not too long," Rebecca said thoughtfully. "The sides of the canyon look ideal for shoring. The actual distance is not too great, either. We might have the bridge built in a month or less, once we started. But there are other costs."

"The lives it would cost building it?" asked Slocum.

"Oh, we don't consider that. No, I meant the maintenance on such a bridge. It is very costly. That's why coming through this canyon would be a better choice."

"It would mean the town of Kennicut dies," Slocum said. "You could run a spur from your main Denver-Santa Fe line and bypass Kennicut entirely."

"So?"

Slocum shook his head. He had seen gunmen who killed without a hint of remorse. Rebecca and her father killed without using a gun, but that didn't mean what they intended for Kennicut—and would do to Bonanza when the silver petered out—did not give exactly the same conclusion.

Rebecca rattled on about profit margins and the cost of rails, how they might buy cheaper grade steel from Pueblo smelters, all manner of minutiae that caused Slocum to drift off. He forced himself back to the real threat facing them when he caught sight of a man riding parallel to the road but trying to avoid being seen by hiding behind trees.

Slocum eased the leather thong off the hammer of his six-shooter to get ready for a fight. He thought he recognized Eachin but was not sure. It hardly mattered who dogged their tracks since they all worked for Malcolm Newcombe.

An uneventful day passed, and they approached the gate leading away from the toll road and on to Bonanza. The only problem after they got through the gate would be getting the wagons up the steep grade to the boom-town.

"Open sesame!" Colonel Simmons cried joyously, waving his arms in front of him as if to part the waters.

Slocum saw that the guards made no move to open the gate. He wondered if they were going to extort more money from Simmons as they had earlier wagon trains. Fighting them off the way Jessup had on the wagon train Slocum and Sarah June had ridden to Bonanza was not likely to happen. Simmons's weapon of choice was money, not bullets.

Right now, Slocum wished they had a few more guns on their side and a little less money.

The guards looked mighty determined not to let Simmons and his men through.

"Who's that?" Slocum asked, seeing a portly man with a bushy handlebar mustache come waddling over from the rebuilt guardhouse. "He looks familiar, but I've never seen him before."

"That's Malcolm Newcombe," Rebecca said with some distaste.

Slocum saw the family resemblance between the elder Newcombe and his son then.

"So, you're Simmons," Malcolm Newcombe said gruffly, stopping in front of the colonel. Newcombe tucked his thumbs in the armholes of his brocade vest.

"You must be Newcombe," answered the railroad magnate. "So good of you to come see us off. A fine toll road you run, sir. A fine one."

"Glad you like it," Newcombe said, pig eyes squinting up at Simmons.

"I like it so well, I want to buy your enterprise. The whole shebang! I'll put you on easy street."

"Can't say I need your money, and the road's not for sale. But I am glad to hear you are so generous. I've been told about that fine coffin of yours."

"What?" Colonel Simmons looked as if someone had stuck a knife into his belly. "What do you mean?"

Rebecca reached over and clutched Slocum's arm. She whispered, "I don't like this."

"I haven't liked it ever since Eachin started trailing us," Slocum said. He glanced over his shoulder and saw Roy Eachin and a dozen guards cutting off any retreat, as if there was anywhere to run back down the canyon. Simmons had to go forward and to do that required passing through the gate.

"I've taken a fancy to your coffin. I figure to accept it in trade for your exit fee."

"Exit fee? Why, that is outrageous, on the face of it, but I will pay."

"Get the coffin, Eachin!" barked Newcombe.

"Wait! I didn't mean you could have it." Simmons paled visibly. "That's my property. You can have any amount you want, but you cannot take the casket. It's mine!"

Simmons's shrill tone only spurred on Malcolm Newcombe. He motioned for Eachin to seize the coffin.

"Stop them!" shrieked Simmons. "Shoot them if they lay one finger on my coffin!" His orders fell on deaf ears. All his men had their hands thrust high, every one of them covered by Newcombe's guards.

"John, you can't let Newcombe take it. My father can't survive without it!" Rebecca looked as frantic as her father.

"It's only a box," Slocum said. "Handing it over to Newcombe means nobody has to use it yet." Slocum figured Newcombe had no real interest in the coffin other than to get Simmons's goat. If Malcolm had wanted to upset the railroad magnate, he had succeeded beyond his wildest dreams.

Rebecca tried to soothe her father, but he pushed her away. Slocum rode to the colonel's side and said in a low voice, "Live to fight again another day. Try to save your coffin and Newcombe will bury you in it."

"I . . . I can get it back later," Simmons said, trying to convince himself this was true. "You can steal it back. I'll post a reward. I'll put a bounty on Newcombe's head! I'll—"

"Do it on the other side of the gate," Slocum urged. He wanted to get out from under the dozen leveled rifles before discussing the matter any further.

Colonel Simmons let out a screech and tried to dive from the saddle and tackle Malcolm Newcombe. Slocum moved faster, his six-gun whipping around and catching the owner of the CGRR on the side of the head. He stunned Simmons enough to drag him back into the saddle. The man sagged but still fought to get at his tormentor. Slocum refused to let Simmons move.

"Take it," Slocum said to Newcombe. "And let us go."

Malcolm Newcombe's mocking laughter followed them through the gate and up the steep slope leading to Bonanza. Rebecca refused to talk to Slocum and her father wept as if he had lost his entire family in a terrible accident.

Slocum was glad they had escaped alive, especially since Eachin had looked as if he intended to gun them down at any instant.

11

"He's a broken man," muttered Rebecca as she rode beside Slocum. On the far side of the remaining wagons Colonel Simmons bobbed disconsolately as his horse walked slowly up the steep slope into Bonanza. Slocum would have thought the railroad magnate was going to his own hanging from the way he looked.

"Newcombe just took his casket, that's all," Slocum said. "He's a rich man. He can build another."

"It's not that simple," Rebecca said.

"I know, the colonel's different from other men." Slocum said in disgust.

"Don't use that tone," Rebecca snapped. "What happens if he dies now? He'll have to be buried in a pine box, if he's lucky. If not, why, he might end up being put down in a grave for the worms to eat with nothing around him."

"I'll donate my saddle blanket." Slocum said. He was fed up with Rebecca and especially the colonel's odd ways. Everyone faced death on the frontier but never had Slocum seen a man so peculiarly obsessed with the notion of needing to bring along his own coffin. He had to hand it to Malcolm Newcombe. The man had masterfully recognized the single item that would destroy his foe. If he had murdered Rebecca in front of Colonel Simmons, the effect could not have been more devastating.

"That was uncalled for," Rebecca said, a flush coming to her cheeks as her anger mounted. "How dare you mock him? He's a great man."

"A great man without his casket." Slocum said, needling her. He regretted it from the way she turned from him and squared her shoulders. The redhead stared straight ahead and rode with lips pulled back into something approaching a snarl.

Slocum was willing to let them work it out on their own. The colonel had buckets of money and toadies in their mock uniforms willing to jump at his every command. Rebecca was the one he could not understand. She was lovely, intelligent, and yet acted in complete subservience to her father.

"Are you going to put up in the Eldorado?" he asked.

"What's it to you?"

Slocum saw a half-dozen wagons parked along Bonanza's main street and saw they had not been loaded with supplies or equipment. That meant a huge influx of miners now sought accommodations throughout the bursting-at-the-seems town.

He waited as Rebecca jumped to the ground and went into the hotel, only to come storming out a few minutes later. She glared up at Slocum as if it were his fault.

"It's full. They are selling sleeping space on the floors! Some rooms have as many as six men in them!"

"Bonanza is a bonanza," he said, using her own phrase. Rebecca got even madder.

"What are you going to do about it? My father needs a place to sleep."

"Reckon the stable is full up, too," Slocum said. He

preferred the clean straw and horses around him to most hotel rooms, but doubted Rebecca or her father would agree. "If he's got enough money, why not buy the hotel and evict the miners?"

"I made an offer," Rebecca said. "They wouldn't sell. In fact, they were quite rude to me."

"Might have something to do with a clerk getting gunned down while you were here."

"Help us, John. You know about such things."

"Wait here and let me see what I can rustle up for you," he said. Slocum rode slowly in the direction of the Tons o' Gold, wondering if Sarah June would even talk to him. He dismounted and went inside. Sarah June was talking to Abel but turned when the barkeep's attention fixed on him. If Slocum was any judge. Sarah June brightened, then hastily covered her reaction to seeing him again.

"You run out of money, Mr. Slocum?" she asked.

"Not exactly," he said. Slocum dropped one of the greenbacks he had been paid by the colonel onto the bar. "Fill up one of those jelly jars," he told Abel.

"Yes, sir!" The young barkeep readily obeyed.

"What brings you back this way?" Sarah June asked.

"I had to look in on you, to see if everything was going well."

"It is," she said, her chocolate-colored eyes fixed on his. He seemed to fall into an endless spiral when he looked at her. She was nowhere as lovely as Rebecca, but there was substance here lacking in the railroad baron's daughter. Slocum wanted to tell her how he had been thinking of her but knew better.

"You know that Colonel Simmons is in town?"

"News travels fast. I heard about the set-to with Malcolm Newcombe. Newcombe is a real son of a bitch."

Slocum didn't want to go into how upset Simmons was over losing his coffin. He didn't even ask how Sarah June had heard the news before the colonel arrived. This was a boomtown and all the miners had to do was work, get drunk, spy on one another, and gossip endlessly. The tidbit about the colonel and Newcombe at the toll road gate had probably earned the man delivering it a free drink.

"The hotel is full, and the colonel doesn't have a place to stay."

"I reckon that lovely little red-haired slip of girl with him has a place to stay," Sarah June said sharply.

Slocum shook his head. "Nope. She needs a place to stay, too. And the others with them." He knew Sarah June thought Rebecca was sharing his blanket. She had, but Slocum wasn't about to tell the saloon owner how he had been thinking of her all the while. Sarah June probably wouldn't believe it. Slocum wasn't sure he would blame her for branding him an outright liar if he did mention it.

"Miss Daniels, we kin put 'em up in the gamblin' tent," Abel said.

"If the price is right," Sarah June added. For a moment, her eyes locked again with Slocum's, making him wonder what the right price might be. The instant passed and Sarah June added, "Two hundred a night to rent the tent."

"I think they can pay more," Slocum said. "I'll see if the colonel won't go for five hundred. What about the gambling?"

Sarah June made a sour face, then sniffed. "Never worked out right, not without you there to oversee the games. I expected the tinhorns to try to cheat me, but they were gypping the miners, too. I won't tolerate that. I might charge them too much for booze and take their money in tips for a few minutes of talk only, but robbing them in a poker game won't happen in the Tons o' Gold!"

Slocum admired her fire and her honesty. He couldn't help comparing this with how Colonel Simmons had boasted of all the ways he intended to cut corners and chisel every dime he could out of Bonanza before letting it rust.

"Don't be too surprised if the colonel sets up in the tent and makes the rest of his men sleep outside," Slocum said.

"Along with his daughter?"

"She might get to sleep at the foot of his bed," Slocum said, deadpan.

For a moment, Sarah June didn't know how to take it. Then she laughed. "You're such a card, John. If you can get that much out of them, I'll give you twenty-five percent."

"The money's yours, Sarah June. I suspect you'll more than earn it." Slocum finished his hefty drink, let it swirl around in his belly and sharpen his senses just a mite, then he left to tell Rebecca he had found a place for her and her father to stay in Bonanza.

He walked back to where the Simmons entourage waited impatiently. Rebecca sat with her father in chairs in front of the hotel. She shot to her feet when she saw him.

"He *must* rest. Have you found a place?"

Slocum explained what he had done. At first Rebecca looked skeptical, then made the best of it.

"An entire tent, one fit for a king," she said, more for her father's benefit than anything else.

Slocum couldn't help thinking it was more fitting for a circus but said nothing.

"Very well. We shall use the tent, provided the noise from the saloon is not too extreme."

"Move the tent a ways off," Slocum said. "I had to haggle a bit with the owner."

"That frowsy Daniels harpy," Rebecca said, looking down her patrician nose at him. "It figures that she would attempt to gouge us."

"She started at a thousand a night." Slocum said to

gauge Rebecca's reaction. From the shock, he knew he could not get this amount for Sarah June. "I convinced her it was to the benefit of her and everyone in Bonanza to let your pa have the tent for half that."

"Very well. You have done well, John. Thank you."

He almost laughed at her but did not. She bustled off to get the colonel's men down to the tent and to set up proper sleeping arrangements for her and her father. Slocum noticed that Rebecca never mentioned him. That suited him fine.

After the colonel and his daughter were secured in the former gambling tent, Slocum strolled into the Tons o' Gold. In the hour or so it had taken to get the Simmonses settled, the saloon had filled up with bawdy miners intent on getting drunk. Slocum stopped one fight as he made his way to the bar.

"Another big one for you, Mr. Slocum?" asked Abel.

"Why not?" He looked around but did not see Sarah June. He asked after her.

"She lit out right after you left. Don't rightly know where she went."

"Does she have a place to sleep in town? A permanent one?" Slocum asked, thinking to see if he could mend some fences with her.

"Can't rightly say. I suppose so. Me, I sleep here under the bar. Guards the stock and I don't have to pay nuthin' for a room."

Slocum finished his drink and left the crowded tent in time to see someone slipping out of the nearby tent where Colonel Simmons had bedded down. The dark figure moved furtively, darting from shadow to shadow and moving away from town. Slocum wondered if thieves had already beset the railroad owner and took out after the hurrying shape, turned formless in the night.

He wasn't working for the colonel any longer, but he

hated seeing anyone robbed while they slept.

As Slocum closed the gap between him and the hurrying figure, he realized he was following Rebecca. He slowed and started to let her go to her midnight assignation when he heard her cry out in rage. His hand flashed to his six-shooter, but he did not draw. Slocum had seen her with Buster Newcombe before and nothing had happened. He doubted it would this time, either.

The only difference was that he was close enough to overhear what they said. Curious, Slocum edged to where he could see Rebecca and Buster standing nose to nose again.

"Give it back," she raged.

"My pa won't ever give it up," Buster said, almost whining like a schoolboy caught cheating. "He said if it was good enough for the colonel, it was good enough for him."

"You know how my father can't stand to be away from the coffin, not even for a few minutes."

"Rebecca, please. I tried to get my father to understand, but he only laughed at me."

"That's because you're such a weakling," Rebecca said. Slocum wondered if she would use her finger like a battering ram against Buster's chest again. She started to, then snorted in disgust and spun around, folding her arms over her chest as if this would shut him out of her world.

"I can't buck my pa. You can't face up to yours, either, can you?" Buster shot back.

"I run the company. He does what I say," Rebecca retorted. Buster wasn't buying that any more than Slocum.

"He says jump and you ask how high. I've seen you when you're around him."

"I want the colonel's coffin back." Rebecca said coldly. "I'll ransom it. How much?"

"I told you, Rebecca. I can't do it. My father won't let

it out of his sight. He's as bad as yours." Buster saw this
wasn't getting anywhere with Rebecca. "Look," he said.
"Build a new coffin. A bigger one, fancier. That ought to
suit the colonel."

"It won't be *his* coffin," Rebecca said.

Slocum slipped away without either of them noticing
as he left them to their argument. From the intense passion
they showed for arguing, they might go long into the
night. For his part, Slocum couldn't figure out what the
connection was between Rebecca Simmons and Buster
Newcombe. It wasn't as bitter as the one between their
fathers, but it was hardly one of love.

Slocum had long since learned some things in the world
didn't have explanations, and he was content to let the
matter lie there. He went back to the Tons o' Gold Saloon
and worked on a special bottle Abel had under the bar.

12

Slocum had no idea how he had gotten so mixed up in Colonel Simmons's affairs. He grabbed for his hat as a gust of wind blowing up out of Knife Canyon tried to rip it from his head. Heaving a deep sigh, he reckoned it had a lot to do with Rebecca and the offer of more money than he could make in a month of Sundays gambling at the Tons o' Gold. Sarah June had not been too happy when he had told her that he was escorting the colonel and his daughter to Kennicut, but she had put on a fake smile and had bought him a going-away drink.

It had tasted like acid on his tongue.

"Mr. Slocum, you figure this is the place to cross?"

"What?" Slocum turned, tugged his hat down a little harder around his ears and faced Colonel Simmons's chief engineer. Marcus O'Brien was a short man, the top of his head hardly coming to Slocum's shoulder. What he lacked in height he made up for in girth. He was built like a barrel, and Slocum could not find a single ounce of fat anywhere. O'Brien was immensely strong, not to mention being a fine construction engineer.

"Here? You reckon we can shove the trestle into the rock and cross here?"

Slocum nodded, his eyes drifting to the far side of the steep canyon.

"Reaching the point where you can put in supports will be a problem," Slocum said. "It'll take a powerful lot of blasting to make a ledge big enough to hold the bridge."

"Won't do it that way," O'Brien said, inching closer. He peered over the edge and didn't show a bit of the vertigo that still plagued Slocum. "See those outcroppings? I can get a crew onto them, we can drill straight down into rock and put the supports into them. Done it before on the colonel's roads up near Pike's Peak."

"I'll leave the engineering to you," Slocum said. He had worked as a powder monkey in a mine for a spell, and had done some hard-rock mining in his day, but putting a bridge over Knife Canyon was beyond his ability to imagine. O'Brien made it sound like something he could do before noon.

"I have to hand it to you," O'Brien said. "Convincing the colonel to put the spur from Kennicut into Bonanza was a fancy bit of footwork."

Slocum's eyes widened slightly. He had done nothing to convince the colonel. It had been Rebecca's doing—and having the colonel's coffin stolen by Malcolm Newcombe. The colonel wanted to get back at the toll road owner and break him for his theft.

"I didn't do much," Slocum said carefully.

"So you're modest, too. Don't be. Not if you stay around this lot. Take credit for everything you can. That's the only way to get ahead." O'Brien looked over the brink again, then scribbled a note to himself on a piece of foolscap using a pencil hardly an inch long.

Slocum wondered if Rebecca had circulated the rumor he had been responsible for getting the railroad magnate to change his mind. The only reason he could see was that it insulated her from obviously being out to destroy the Newcombes. Did it have something to do with Buster Newcombe? Rebecca could always claim Slocum had been the one egging the colonel on, but what did she care?

Slocum pushed it out of his mind. For what the Colorado Grand Mountain Railroad was paying him, they could blame Lincoln's assassination on him and he wouldn't much care.

"By the way, Miss Simmons wanted you to report to the colonel's parlor car right away. Something big's in the works."

"All right." Slocum was glad to back away from the edge of the canyon and return to Kennicut a hundred yards off. The solid rock under his feet reassured him that he wasn't going to plunge down a thousand feet into a rocky gorge. He hopped onto the rear step leading into the parlor car—the one where the Colonel had so recently transported his coffin. Slocum knocked sharply on the door, wondering if he ought to go slowly or simply barge in.

Rebecca opened the door. She scowled at him and impatiently waved him into the car. Slocum felt more at ease with the coffin gone. The car no longer seemed so tiny.

"What kept you?" she asked without preamble. "Never mind." Rebecca said, waving her hand as if to dismiss any feeble excuse he might conjure up. "I received word that it is ready. I want you to go to Denver immediately and escort it back here."

"It?"

She looked at him as if he had turned into the village idiot. Rebecca sniffed indignantly and said, "My father's coffin. His *new* coffin."

Slocum refrained from asking if she had taken Buster Newcombe's advice about getting a new one built or if this was simply a spare the colonel had laying around some warehouse.

"You want me to ride shotgun on it?" The notion struck Slocum as funny, but his laugh died when he saw that Rebecca considered this a matter of extreme gravity.

"Do not let it fall into . . . enemy hands."

He didn't have to ask whom she thought the enemy was.

"When do you want me to go?"

"Right away. My father is resting. You can ride the engine to Denver. The train will bring back freight cars with everything Mr. O'Brien needs to build his bridge and lay the track from Kennicut to Bonanza."

"And one car will have the second coffin in it," Slocum finished. Rebecca nodded briskly, obviously dismissing him. He wondered if he ought to say something more, or even try to get a good-bye kiss from the fiery redhead. From the rigid set to her shoulders and the way she looked like a thunderstorm waiting to happen, he decided he would rather kiss a prickly pear.

"Sign here and here," the bored clerk said as Slocum scrawled his name repeatedly on the bottoms of the invoices. "And there." An ink-stained finger stabbed down on a third sheet.

"Any more?"

"Nope, that'll do it. The, uh, package is all yours."

Slocum looked up at the sealed freight car carrying the colonel's new coffin. The car was placed immediately behind a mail car with a large vault holding enough money to pay a railroad crew for a month. Slocum didn't notice any guards in the car, but there had to be a few. Behind the freight car carrying the coffin stretched a dozen more flatcars loaded with steel rails and structural wooden beams needed for the bridge. Slocum had wondered why

Simmons intended shipping the beams until he remembered how bare the mountains around Kennicut were. Over the prior year the miners had cut every available tree to use as shoring for their own mines. No tree taller than a sturdy shrub remained, forcing Simmons to bring in his own wood beams.

He went to the car and tugged on the door. It was fastened with a piece of wire, both ends of which were run through a piece of lead that had been crushed down to secure it. Slocum started to pull it off, then reconsidered. Going to the end of the freight car, he scrambled up the steel rung ladder to the roof. It took him a couple minutes to find a loose board and pry it up so he could drop into the freight car's dark, cool interior.

Slocum heaved a deep sigh of resignation when he saw the coffin in the middle of the freight car. It had been lashed down securely. He ran his fingers over the fancy polished mahogany and touched the precious gems embedded in the lid and sides. If he had wanted to look inside, he would have had to untie the ropes securing it to rings mounted in the floor.

A moment's fancy came and went. Slocum shook his head at the odd notion of opening the coffin and riding to Kennicut inside it. That was something Colonel Simmons might do. Slocum knew when he was put into the ground, it wouldn't be in a fancy casket like this. If he was lucky, he might get a funeral and a spot in a boot hill overlooking some dismal, windswept plain.

He settled down in the corner of the freight car and drifted off to sleep, only to be awakened a half hour later when the train pulled out of Denver, heading back to Kennicut.

Slocum slept fitfully as the rocking motion of the train kept him off-balance and unable ever to get soundly to sleep. He wished he had brought a blanket to cushion the hard floor, but he had been rushed out of Kennicut to fetch the coffin and had left most of his belongings behind. He stretched, yawned, and then cried out when the world turned upside down around him amid sickening, metallic grinding.

The car lurched to the side, then went in the other direction—and kept rolling. Slocum slammed into the wall of the freight car, then tumbled to the roof and back down the other side. Somewhere along the way, he found himself flung out into bright sunlight. Then the world faded as pain hit him like a sledgehammer.

He fought to keep from passing out. In the distance he heard horrible creaking and squealing as tortured metal bent and broke. Then there was only silence. Slocum coughed as clouds of dust billowed up. He wiped as much out of his eyes as he could and struggled to stand. His legs felt like water and his chest ached with every breath.

Slocum went cold inside when he saw what had happened. The engine had derailed and continued rolling, but off the track. Immediately behind it, the mail car had broken its connector and flipped onto its side. His car was next in line and had been thrown from the tracks and had rolled over and over downhill into a ravine. If he had not been tossed out, he might have been crushed inside. There was hardly kindling left of the sturdy freight car. Two other flatcars were twisted about, but remained upright. A few of the flatcars at the rear of the train remained on the tracks, along with the upright caboose.

Limping slightly, Slocum made his way up the hillside to the train. The engineer in the cab had been killed along with his fireman. From the amount of blood he saw dripping from the mail car, the guards inside had not fared well, either. As he started prying his way through the banged-up side of the car to look for survivors, Slocum heard hooves pounding hard.

He jumped to the side of the overturned mail car and saw four masked riders making a beeline for the freight car he had so luckily escaped from. Slocum looked around and saw the crewmen in the caboose weren't going to do anything. They were either too stunned by the accident or had better sense than he did.

Slocum whipped out his Colt Navy, jumped down, and skidded back down the slope to stop the men from stealing Colonel Simmons's coffin.

Three men tore frantically at the crumbled side of the car and unearthed the coffin. Two got behind it and grunted with effort as they pushed it out of the debris. The third man tugged at it.

Slocum considered the thieves, then turned his six-gun on the mounted man. At about the time Slocum sighted along the blued barrel of his pistol, he was distracted by the rattle of a wagon coming along the bottom of the ravine. He glanced over his shoulder and saw a man whipping a team pulling a buckboard.

"It's the guard!" shouted the mounted man, going for his six-shooter when he spotted Slocum. He got off a shot and then flew from the saddle as Slocum's more accurate round caught the man in the middle of the chest. The three men tussling with the coffin stopped and went for their own guns. The air filled with flying lead, forcing Slocum to take cover.

He tried to get a shot at the wagon driver but was kept down by the steady barrage from the other thieves. Slocum chanced a quick glance, saw the three men wrestling the coffin into the buckboard, and then lighting out for their horses. When they ran for it, he had a chance to shoot again. He fired until his six-shooter came up empty and wasn't sure if he had winged any of them.

The wagon lumbered off as the three riders hung back to protect its departure.

Colonel Simmons's coffin had been stolen out from under him. It had taken a derailment—and Slocum had to think that was not accidental—to do it, but he had been entrusted to deliver the box. And he wasn't going to give up.

He caught up the reins of the fourth robber's horse, gentled it a mite, then swung into the saddle. A rifle rode at his knee. It would have to do since he didn't have the ammo to reload his Colt Navy. With a snap of the reins and sharp kicks to the horse's flanks, he raced off after the coffin thieves, determination burning brightly.

13

The robbers traveled along the rocky ravine until they reached a road a quarter mile off from where they had wrecked the train. Slocum saw the direction they took on the road and cut off at an angle across the plains to get ahead of them. The outlaw's horse he rode was no match to his accustomed mare and flagged quickly under the relentless pace. Slocum ruthlessly pushed it to the limits of endurance and got to the road before the robbers.

He hit the ground running, letting the horse stumble away as he yanked the rifle from the saddle holster. Slocum's bruised and battered legs almost betrayed him. He fell, then stood, wondering at his momentary weakness. For the first time since the wreck, he looked down. His jeans were ripped and bloody from the beating he had taken. Slocum knew he had to pick out splinters from his flesh and stanch some of the bleeding, but would do it later.

After he got the colonel's coffin back.

"His damned coffin," Slocum muttered as he levered a round into the rifle's chamber, and he dropped to his belly so he could sight down the road.

He waited less than five minutes for the three bandits and their wagon to come clanking up. Slocum knew he lacked the ammunition to fight a prolonged battle with the men. They had seen fit to murder the train crew to rob the train, so he figured he was acting not only in self-defense, but also as an agent of the court when he squeezed back on the trigger. The rifle bucked into his shoulder, and one bandit threw up his arms before tumbling from the saddle.

The other two riders looked around frantically as they tried to find the hidden sniper. Slocum took out the driver next. He had been hired to deliver the casket and dared not let the man simply drive away while his two partners fought it out.

"There!" shouted one rider, pointing to the wrong side of the road. "I see him!"

The two remaining riders began filling a patch of prickly pear cactus with enough lead to kill a man a dozen times over. Slocum waited until both men's guns came up empty before showing himself.

"Throw down your irons," he shouted. They jerked around, startled as they saw him for the first time.

One lifted his six-shooter, but Slocum warned him off. "You're out of ammo. Don't make me kill you like you killed the train crew."

The man hesitated, then read death in Slocum's eyes. He dropped his six-gun. Slocum turned his rifle toward the second robber, who followed suit reluctantly.

"Who sent you to steal the colonel's coffin?" Slocum asked. He edged over to the buckboard and checked to be sure the driver was dead. The man lay on his back, half-sprawled over the flashy coffin. Slocum grabbed a handful of shirt and yanked hard enough to drag the man out of the wagon and onto the ground. It wouldn't do having the casket drenched in blood before the colonel received it.

The men didn't answer. Slocum had not expected them to.

"Did Eachin send you? This is something he'd think up. Or was it Malcolm Newcombe himself?"

Slocum saw he had touched a nerve when he mentioned Newcombe. He clambered into the buckboard and caught up the reins, wondering what he was going to do with two prisoners. Shooting them in cold blood appealed to him, but he couldn't quite bring himself to do it. There had been enough bloodshed for today.

Even worse, it had been over a casket.

"If you try to get away, I'll shoot you out of the saddle," Slocum told them.

"Where are we going?" asked one.

"Back to the train," he said, not knowing where they were along the route. From the look of the mountains to the west, they were past Pueblo already and angling southwest toward Kennicut. That meant they were miles from any town, much less one with a marshal and a jail for these murderous owlhoots.

Slocum considered making the men walk to keep them from bolting, but he knew that would take forever to return to the railroad tracks. He drove cautiously as he kept the men's backs in sight. Slocum expected them to try to escape as they rode up the ravine near the tracks, but the two were subdued. Slocum reined back when they reached the freight car that had once rolled along with the coffin in it.

"Whoa, boys," he called. "You two are going to carry the coffin back to the train."

"Up there? I'd sooner die than . . ." The man's voice trailed off when he saw that was his only alternative. Either carry the coffin or end up with a bullet in his belly. The two men grunted, cursed and struggled to get the casket back to the train.

To Slocum's surprise, the engine was sitting upright back on the tracks and a crew worked diligently to repair the rail loosened by the robbers.

"What you got there, Slocum?" called Marcus O'Brien. The short engineer ambled over and eyed the prisoners with a gimlet eye. "They do the damage?"

"They're the only ones who lived to brag about it," Slocum said.

"It doesn't look like they're doing much bragging right now," O'Brien said, grinning.

"How'd you happen to come along with all that equipment?" Slocum stared at the winches and cranes finishing their work of lifting the heavy steam engine back onto the tracks. "I would have bet a hundred dollars that engine would never have been set on the tracks any time soon."

"This happens all the time," O'Brien said. "Narrow gauge trains are lighter and easier to wrestle back than the bigger, standard gauge ones: But you got lucky. Colonel Simmons sent me out to scout the train on a handcar. I saw what happened and got the rescue crew out right away. The colonel *really* wants to push that spur across to Bonanza."

Slocum took a minute to look around and saw that what O'Brien said could have happened. They were closer to Kennicut than he would have guessed from his time in the freight car.

"Reckon I slept more than I thought," Slocum said ruefully.

"You weren't asleep when those gents came to steal the coffin."

"Might be more to their mischief," Slocum said. He turned grim when he saw three of the colonel's men finishing graves for the engineer, fireman, and a mail car guard alongside the tracks. It was a fitting spot to rest for a railroad man, but the men should never have died.

Not for a coffin.

"You thinking what I am? That Newcombe wants to stop the bridge from ever being built?" O'Brien shrugged his broad shoulders. "I've fought against worse than him."

"The railroad spur will make his toll road worthless," Slocum said. Then he pictured Knife Canyon in his mind and knew O'Brien had a potent foe to fight other than Malcolm Newcombe.

"When can we get rolling?" Slocum asked.

"Got to build up a head of steam in the boiler, then it's a piece of cake." O'Brien waved to his engineer, who hopped down and went to the newly positioned locomotive on its replaced track. "I'll let Stanley steam you on into Kennicut. He's a topnotch engineer."

"What about a fireman?"

"Well, I intend to highball into Kennicut and I haven't spent twenty years working my way up to stoke coal. And I don't think it's possible to get any of the men in the caboose to stoke for you." O'Brien fixed his steely gaze on Slocum.

"The colonel's paying me well," Slocum said. "Shoveling coal for a spell won't hurt me."

"You said you slept most of the way here. You're rested and ready," said O'Brien, laughing as he slapped Slocum on the shoulder. The construction engineer set off to get into the caboose. Slocum climbed into the cab and looked around. Sitting on a drop seat, Stan worked his way through the gauges and pulled levers.

"You gonna fire for me?"

"That wasn't my first choice," Slocum said honestly, hanging his gun belt on a rod and rolling up his sleeves. "But you got me, for better or worse. What do I do?"

"Start stoking. It's gonna take awhile 'fore I get a head of steam built again. Danged lucky the boiler didn't pop when the engine left the tracks." Stan canted his head to one side and peered at Slocum. "If you see any rivets shakin', you tell me right away."

"Or we're likely to explode?"

"Somethin' like that," Stan said, moping his face with a grimy rag. "You catch on fast."

Slocum began stoking the firebox, but kept a wary eye on the bolts and rivets festooning the cab. Before he knew it, the train had steamed into Kennicut. The real work of building the bridge across Knife Canyon lay ahead.

14

Slocum sat on a large wind-smoothed rock a few feet from the abrupt verge and marveled at how quickly Marcus O'Brien had constructed the bridge. The skeleton structure had gone up within a week of Slocum bringing in the supply train—with Colonel Simmons's new coffin—and after that work had gone even faster. In a way, Slocum thought the colonel getting his fancy casket helped the most to speed things along. The Colorado Grand Mountain Railroad owner had become more animated, made decisions easily, and demonstrated how he had built an empire of steel rails rivaling General Palmer and the other narrow-gauge railroad barons in Colorado.

The sounds of blasting and drilling echoed up from the sheer side of the canyon, but Slocum still heard the soft crunch of shoes on gravel behind him. He turned to see Rebecca Simmons coming up the road from Kennicut.

"I wondered where you spent your days," she said. "You've been a stranger lately."

"I'd only be in the way back in town. You and the colonel have been working long hours getting that built." Slocum pointed to the bridge. The last of the braces across the top were being nailed into place. It would be only a matter of days before the steel rails were put into place and the construction on the other side through Markam Pass into Bonanza could begin.

"You're not in the way," she said, sitting beside him. Slocum remembered all he had seen in the fiery redhead before. She had become vibrant and alive again and not the disagreeable harpy she had been in Bonanza. Slocum could not help recollecting how she and Buster Newcombe had stood nose to nose arguing.

"I do what I can, but O'Brien and his crew are doing all the work."

"You brought in two of the men who tried to steal the colonel's coffin," Rebecca said, color coming to her bone-china-pale cheeks. "The ones you didn't take prisoner, you shot." A tinge of bitterness shaded her voice, reminding Slocum of what Rebecca could be. He looked across Knife Canyon with some anticipation. He wanted to be on the first train rumbling over the gulch and on into Bonanza. That was still weeks off, but Slocum wanted to stand tall in the cab beside the engineer so he could wave to the crowd in Bonanza.

From that vantage point he could see if Sarah June Daniels was there to greet him.

"I'm glad the sheriff decided to send the pair of them back to Denver. Did he ever find out if they worked for Newcombe?"

"What's the difference?" she asked sharply. Something about the way Rebecca spat out the words told Slocum she knew more about the attempted hijacking of the casket than she was telling. Since she did not venture a more complete report to him, he figured it meant Buster Newcombe had been responsible for sending out the robbers. That was about all he could think that would gall Rebecca so she wouldn't vent her anger openly. She and Buster shared more with each other than they did with the world around them.

Slocum knew the woman's hot temper was always boiling just below her placid, lovely exterior. He wondered if the same was true of Buster.

"Doesn't matter," he said, knowing it did to the woman. "My job doesn't amount to much since I caught them. I've been thinking about moving on again."

"No, John, you can't! We still need you," she said, startled at such a possible defection. Her emerald eyes fixed on him and she said in a low, husky whisper, "I need you."

He almost laughed in her face. Rebecca didn't need him or anything else but the Colorado Grand Mountain Railroad. No man could match the thrill she experienced planning and plotting the course of this vital business.

"I'll double what you're getting."

Slocum had to think on this. Even bucking the tiger for a successful keno game in the Tons o' Gold over in Bonanza—if Sarah June would even let him back into her saloon—would not make that kind of money in a month of Sundays.

"Why am I so valuable?" he asked.

"I . . . I fear there might be attempts to destroy the bridge. We need someone watching constantly, someone we trust. Just as you are doing now, without being told." She laid her hand on his arm and squeezed lightly. "Can we count on you?"

"For a while longer," Slocum said. "I want to ride across O'Brien's bridge, though."

"Good! That will make a splendid bonus!" she exclaimed. Rebecca shot to her feet. "I have to get back to town. The Pueblo smelters are trying to simply *rob* us on what they charge for rails." She bustled off, muttering to herself about profit margins and returns on investment. Slocum looked back at the bridge.

He heaved to his feet and went to see what he could find. If he was responsible for protecting the bridge, he wanted to know its weaknesses as well as its strengths.

The cold wind whipped down off the top of the canyon rim and sought to insinuate icy fingers under Slocum's jacket. He shivered and pulled the coat tighter around him. Then he blew on his hands and rubbed them together to keep the circulation flowing. Although it was well into May, winter refused to surrender to warmer temperatures, at least this high up in the mountains.

Slocum looked down at the base of the bridge where O'Brien had driven the posts directly into the stubborn rock. It was nothing short of an engineering—mining—marvel. If he had built ledges to support the base of the trestle, he might still be working. As it was, the train would rattle its way over Knife Canyon in a couple days on its way with supplies to the crew laying track through Markam Pass. Slocum intended to be on the train. It was his due, his reward for freezing to death so many nights protecting the bridge.

"Protecting it from nothing," he grumbled. He had spent a full week patrolling the rim, then had decided to descend a ways on the supports during his watch to be certain the base was intact. In all that time, he hadn't seen anything but a couple cougars and a half-dozen coyotes coming to camp to eat garbage.

Slocum huddled down against the cold rock, seeking some protection from the omnipresent wind. It took him a few minutes to figure out what wasn't right. The timbers in the bridge creaked and moaned as they were buffeted by the wind but the vibration through the rock alerted Slocum that trouble was brewing.

He stood and looked up along the supports at the bridge, then began climbing. The construction crew had chewed hard- and footholds out of the sheer rock, making it easier for him to climb. He got to the top and saw two dark figures silhouetted against the starry night sky above him. Slocum hefted his rifle and started to take aim, then settled down. O'Brien might be restless about finishing the bridge and had ventured out to inspect it with an assistant.

But the men lacked the calm assurance the project engineer did when crossing the bridge. Slocum respected the way O'Brien ignored the steep precipices and dizzying heights. These men acted more like Slocum himself, wary of making a misstep rather than being confident of their footing.

"Put it here and let's go," one said to the other.

"Here? It won't do any good putting it here. We got to take out one of the supports. I tell you, blowing the middle of the bridge ain't as good as going for the base."

"You ain't gettin' me to climb down there! Not in the dark!"

Slocum made his way along the rim, gingerly stepping out on the crossties that would take steel rails in another day or two.

"Can I help you gents?" Slocum asked.

Both men jumped as if they were stung by ants. One teetered and almost went over the edge of the bridge, but the other knelt. A bright flash warned Slocum the man had struck a lucifer. The man who had almost lost his balance moved to block the other from his sight, but Slocum knew the second man was lighting a fuse.

"Stay where you are or I'll shoot!" he called.

"Come on, Murdoch!" The one standing scrambled over his partner, who still knelt. Slocum saw the fitful sputter of miner's black fuse but didn't see what it led to.

There was no reason to believe it was anything other than a bundle of dynamite, though.

Murdoch forced Slocum to stop in his tracks when he opened fire. A foot-long orange flame blasted from the muzzle of the bomber's six-shooter. Where the slug went Slocum didn't know. Murdoch had missed him by a country mile in the dark. Slocum was a better shot and had the muzzle flash to help him aim. He fired.

For a moment he didn't know if he had hit the man. Murdoch rose to full height and turned slightly.

"Go on, Jed," Murdoch said in a strong voice. Then he toppled like a felled tree, hitting the side of the bridge and falling over the edge. If Slocum's bullet hadn't killed him, the fall would.

"Murdoch! You kilt Murdoch!" shrieked Jed, now half-way across the trestle. Slocum drew his rifle snugly against his shoulder again and fired a second time. This time he missed. Jed fired wildly, his six-shooter spitting eye-dazzling tongues of fire in Slocum's direction.

Slocum grunted when one bullet found his right thigh. He reached down involuntarily. His fingers came away wet with his own blood. More angry than hurt, he put his bloody finger back onto the trigger and sighted in on the now retreating back. Jed was three-quarters of the way across the bridge when the dynamite went off.

The entire structure shuddered as if it had the croup. Slocum stumbled and fell to one knee. His rifle tumbled over the side into the black maw of Knife Canyon. But he didn't care about losing his Winchester. He was more concerned with his own life. The bridge screamed like an animal caught in a trap as it twisted and began to buck.

Slocum saw the man who had helped plant the bomb throw up his hands and then follow his partner into oblivion. That was cold comfort for Slocum though. The bridge was sagging forward toward the spot where the bomb had gone off, taking him with it. Slocum clutched fiercely to the wood and found a secure support.

He tried pulling himself back toward the safety of the rocky canyon lip where the bridge started when another section gave way. Slocum held on firmly to a piece of wood that had broken loose and was slipping into the canyon. He abandoned his grip on the sliding wood and scrambled fast, trying to find purchase for the toes of his boots. He struck a rock and thought he was safe. Then the rock gave way, and Slocum continued his delayed fall into the deadly, deep canyon.

Twisting hard, he rolled and, flat on his back, grabbed another beam that wasn't moving. Slocum kicked and got his legs wrapped around the support and finally rolled on top of it. The rest of the trestle was vanishing around him, leaving only the single, foot-wide beam. He clung to it, then got to his feet and balanced carefully as he made his way to safety.

Slocum didn't stop when he got to solid ground but kept walking until he reached a spot many yards from the bridge. Only then did he sink to the ground, gasping for air. The panic finally hit him. His heart raced and then settled down as a cold calm enveloped him. Slocum flopped over and sat so he could look out over the bridge.

Or what remained of it. The dynamite had blown away one half of the bridge, leaving the rest—the part Slocum had walked over to safety—precariously swaying in the wind.

Slocum had got to his feet and dusted himself off by the time O'Brien and his crew came running up.

"What happened?" demanded the engineer. "I heard a blast, sounded like five sticks of dynamite, and came running."

"You heard right," Slocum said grimly. "The dynamite might be the next round in the fight." He left the engineer fretting and fussing over saving what he could of his trestle and went to find Rebecca and her father.

15

Slocum had not thought O'Brien could rebuild the bridge as fast as he had. From the damage done by the bomb, Slocum figured it would be a week or more. O'Brien had finished the work in three days. Slocum had stood guard, even patrolling Kennicut at night hunting for Newcombe's men, but had heard only rumors of them drifting through town. One miner had described Roy Eachin well enough to put Slocum on edge, but Newcombe's henchman proved to be a will-o'-the-wisp. Slocum had hunted but never caught sight of Eachin.

O'Brien stomped over to where Slocum watched the last nails being driven into the repaired bridge and looked up at him. A sparkle in his eyes told Slocum the job was finished.

"You ready to ride the train?"

"Across the bridge?" asked Slocum.

"All the way into Bonanza. The extra days we spent fixing the damage gave the crew up in Markam Pass time to lay tracks."

Slocum knew a considerable amount of rail had been moved across the bridge while it was under construction, but had not realized there had been enough to complete the railroad spur.

"I see what you're thinking, Slocum," O'Brien said, moving closer. "Truth is, we cut some corners. Some big ones. The trip won't be too safe until a crew re-lays the tracks, but it'll be good enough for one grand gesture."

"To Bonanza," Slocum said, willing to take the risk of derailment to get out of Kennicut. The chance to see Sarah June again entered into it, too.

It took four hours to get the colonel's special train off the siding and onto the tracks leading across the bridge. Slocum stood next to O'Brien and the engineer in the cab while Colonel Simmons and Rebecca made speeches off the rear platform of the car carrying the man's coffin. Even over the chuffing of the steam engine and the applause of the crowd Slocum heard Simmons's booming voice predicting future success for the people of Kennicut and a new era of prosperity for all Colorado.

"He should have been a politician." Slocum said.

O'Brien laughed. "What makes you think he isn't?" The short man swung out and hung like a monkey on the side of the engine cab. The brass band struck up a tune and O'Brien got the high sign from someone in the crowd. He pointed his pudgy finger across the bridge.

The train engineer slammed home a lever, released a blast of steam through the whistle, and the train lurched forward. Slocum caught his breath as the engine rolled onto the creaking bridge. For a heartstopping instant Slocum thought the trestle was crumbling under the weight. Then he realized it was only the wood compressing. The structure held as the train crossed the span of Knife Canyon and reached the far side. From behind came a huge cheer from the crowd. Then it died down as the train curled around a bend and into the hills going into Markam Pass.

The trip that had taken Slocum days passed in hours on the train. In spite of O'Brien's cautions, the rails held and the train highballed through the pass and down the slope toward Bonanza. Slocum squinted into the wind and cinders pelting him as he searched the gathered crowd looking for Sarah June. He didn't see her.

The train whistled its way into Bonanza, screeching to a stop in the center of the gathered miners. The noise of the train had been deafening during the trip. It was nothing compared to the shouts of the crowd welcoming them. Again, Colonel Simmons launched into his speech and drew the bulk of the miners.

"Well done," O'Brien said, shaking Slocum's hand.

"I could say the same. You worked miracles."

"Of course I did," O'Brien said, grinning ear to ear. "It's what I do!"

Slocum jumped to the ground and made his way around the edge of the crowd. He had no reason to listen to more of Colonel Simmons's harangue about how this was a new day and prosperity was going to be delivered every time a Colorado Grand Mountain Railroad train pulled into Bonanza. But as he made his way toward the Tons o' Gold Saloon, Slocum saw considerable destruction. Buildings had burned to the ground. Those that still stood had bullet holes in the walls. Glass windows, what few there had been, were broken and boarded over. It looked as if a major battle had been fought in Bonanza.

Broken glass grinding under his boots, Slocum left the main street and went behind buildings to the flapping tent over the saloon. He expected most of the townspeople to be gathered to welcome the colonel. It surprised him to find a dozen men crowded into the Tons o' Gold, all drinking in silence.

"Hey, Mr. Slocum. Welcome back. Never thought I'd lay eyes on you again." Abel reached under the bar and pulled out a bottle filled with amber liquid. Calling it liquor was beyond Slocum's capacity for lying to himself. He sampled the shot Abel poured and made a face.

"With the train making regular runs, you can get real tarantula juice."

"If there's anybody left," Abel said, his smile fading. He looked around the saloon, then poured another shot for Slocum.

"Where's Sarah June?"

"Miss Daniels is prob'ly watchin' the colonel."

"I didn't see her."

"Big crowd." Abel turned more taciturn, and Slocum knew he had to ask fast or he wouldn't learn what was going on in Bonanza—and with Sarah June.

"The town looks like a gang of cowboys hurrahed it. What happened?"

"The war," Abel said. "It's splittin' us apart something fierce. Good friends are shootin' at us now. All because of the colonel and Newcombe."

"That seems incredible," Slocum said. "Who'd support Newcombe and his toll road? The man is an outright crook."

"It might seem incredible, but it's true," came a voice Slocum remembered well. He turned to face Sarah June. She was a vision of loveliness. "Newcombe has money enough to buy an army. And he did. It's killing business—and Bonanza."

"You've got enough men in here to pay the rent," Slocum said, indicating the miners slowly savoring their rotgut.

"Didn't Abel tell you? If a miner's leaving town, we give them a free going-away drink."

"They're all leaving?"

"Yep, that's so," Abel said. "Them that don't want to fight to save their claims or those whose claims ain't so good are all hightailin' it. Newcombe gives 'em free passage out."

"How free?" Slocum asked Sarah June, suspecting there was more to it than Abel allowed.

"He takes the deed to their claims," she said. "He's gobbling up as much land as he can. Not all of it is any good, but some is. Enough."

"Who shot up Bonanza?"

"Everyone, no one," Sarah June said in dejection. "The lines have been drawn. You're either for Newcombe and his toll road or for Colonel Simmons and his train. Nobody is neutral."

"You're not?" Slocum began to worry. Sarah June looked distraught, and he wondered if there was more involved than simply watching Bonanza pulled apart by a war between Newcombe and Simmons.

"I have to back Simmons. There was no other choice since Newcombe cut off all my supplies. He saw how profitable the Tons o' Gold was becoming and decided to move in on me."

"He didn't hurt you?" The edge in Slocum's voice brought Sarah June around. She looked at him hard.

"I'm all right, John. Thank you for asking, though."

A ruckus outside drew his attention. Slocum went to the tent flap and looked out on a melee in progress. Miners swung ax handles and others—possibly Newcombe's men—fought back with even more dangerous implements. The roar of a shotgun brought a loud screech of pain.

"They're killin' us!"

"Go back over the mountains, railroad thief!" someone cried. This got the crowd riled even more. The fight looked as if it would engulf Bonanza and bring down the flimsy buildings. Slocum got to the train and shouted at

Marcus O'Brien. "Get your men. We have to push New-combe's gang out of town!"

O'Brien didn't need any urging. His deep voice boomed like a bass drum and brought forth a dozen burly men from his railroad crew, all carrying pry bars and rail-road spikes as weapons. They jumped into the fray and soon pushed back Newcombe's men and supporters to the edge of Bonanza. Once that far, Newcombe's men turned tail and ran.

"After 'em!" shouted O'Brien before Slocum could caution him not to follow. Newcombe's men ran for the safety of the toll road and its fortifications. From the guardhouses at the mouth of the canyon, Newcombe could hold off an army—especially one armed only with clubs.

Slocum ran hard and caught up with O'Brien and shouted at him. "Stop them. Newcombe will cut them down." He pointed to the blockhouse bristling with rifle barrels.

"Hold on, men," O'Brien bellowed. His command cut through the angry cries and clatter of clubs smashing into bodies. "Get on back here. It's a trap!"

The fight deteriorated then, Newcombe's men seeking safety behind the barbed wire fences and those from Bo-nanza moving away warily. Slocum saw a man struggling to get to the upper wall of one blockhouse. Precariously balanced, Malcolm Newcombe laughed at the miners and railroad workers who had chased his henchmen.

"You're gonna get cut off! I'm stopping all your sup-plies!" Newcombe shouted, using his cupped hands as a megaphone. "There won't be a crumb arriving from the outside. Starve! Starve or throw in with me!"

"He wants our claims," whined one miner.

"There's no need to lament," came a voice as powerful as Newcombe's. Riding on a stallion, Colonel Simmons trotted to the gate and looked up at his foe. "The Colorado

Grand Mountain Railroad will supply Bonanza from now on. There's no need for a toll road." The way Simmons spat out the last two words made them sound like cuss words.

The colonel wheeled his horse around so he faced Newcombe. "As for you, you miserable worm, I'll bring in enough men to tear down your pitiful fence and burn your guardhouses unless you return my property immediately!"

Many miners in the crowd looked at each other, not knowing what Simmons meant. Slocum knew. Simmons wanted his coffin back. In spite of having a fancy new casket, it wasn't the same. He had to force Newcombe to return his coffin or lose face.

"Open fire!" shouted Newcombe.

Slocum and O'Brien got the crowd away from the mouth of the canyon before Newcombe's men had the chance to cut down many of them. Colonel Simmons sat on his horse like a statue, unmoving and unmoved. He finally snorted in contempt and rode off, his back a target for any of Newcombe's snipers. If any of the men tried to bushwhack him, they failed. Simmons rode among the miners and railroad workers and assembled them.

"Fight that swine. Fight him and anyone in Bonanza sympathizing with him. To the death!"

With a roar, the miners charged back to Bonanza, ready to kill anyone not openly supporting Simmons and this railroad.

"This is getting out of hand," Slocum said. "It's got to stop or men will start dying by the bucketful."

O'Brien shook his head. "I'm not happy about it, Slocum, but I work for the colonel. I do what he says, even if it is wrong." With that, O'Brien trudged off to join the crowd. Slocum hoped the construction engineer had enough control over his crew to keep them from wanton killing.

But he doubted it.

Angling away from the route taken by the crowd, Slocum headed for the train. He found Rebecca in the last car, staring at the coffin as if she wondered what might be inside it. She looked up with distant eyes when he entered.

"What is it, John?"

"You've got to talk to your pa and stop the killing. He told the crowd to slaughter anyone in Bonanza supporting Newcombe."

"So?"

"This isn't the way to get the other coffin back. It's all about that coffin, isn't it? Everything the colonel has done has been aimed at forcing Newcombe to give it back."

"People die all the time," Rebecca said, color coming to her pale cheeks. "Why do you care a whit for Newcombe or any of his men?"

"I don't," Slocum said. "I don't want to see any of the miners hurt. They don't know how to fight. They dig in the ground for silver and gold for a living."

"They should fight for what's theirs," she said. "My father's committing our rail workers to the fight. Should the people of Bonanza do less?"

"This is crazy," Slocum said. "It's one thing to fight over money, trade, keeping an entire boomtown supplied so it can grow. But this fight's personal between the colonel and Newcombe. And it's all about a damned coffin!"

"Excuse me. I want to be sure none of Newcombe's men escapes." Rebecca pushed past Slocum, and he knew then that total war had been declared. Neither the Newcombes nor the Simmonses would be content until the other side was obliterated.

It was time for Slocum to get the hell out of Bonanza—after he convinced Sarah June to come with him.

16

Slocum found himself dodging from building to rock to shrub, sometimes even wriggling on his belly like a snake to avoid the snipers shooting at anything that moved. Rebecca and her father had fired up the miners something fierce. They shot at shadows and each other. Whether they hit any of Newcombe's men was beside the point. They were scared and getting more frightened by the minute.

In that, Slocum couldn't fault them. He was afraid the war building in the small town was beyond anyone's control now. What angered him more than anything else was the coffin. It was partly a feud over supplying Bonanza and the surroundings but it seemed to him more of a fight to get Colonel Simmons's coffin back. He had seen men die for stupid causes, but this was about the dumbest reason for catching a slug in the belly that Slocum had ever heard.

The Tons o' Gold Saloon flapped ahead of him. The miners inside had long since left. Slocum raced the last few yards and dived into the tent. He heaved a sigh of relief and looked around, wondering where Abel had gone. Then Slocum realized Abel was not a stupid man.

He was hiding where he wouldn't get shot.

As a slug ripped through the canvas and sailed a foot over Slocum's head, he knew this was the place to be, also. In hiding.

"Sarah June!" he called. "Where are you? Are you all right?"

Slocum poked around behind the bar, ducking involuntarily when another bullet broke a bottle of rye whiskey next to him. Newcombe and Simmons had their war going full tilt now. He had hoped Rebecca would talk some sense into her pa, but she was as crazy as he was.

"Sarah June!"

Slocum spotted a foot sticking out from under a large box. He used the bar he had built as protection from the gunfire and rushed to the crate that had toppled from a pile taller than his head. Slocum threw the box off and saw the brunette laying facedown on the ground. He gently rolled her over, fearing the worse.

Her eyelids fluttered and brown eyes gradually focused. "John?"

"Come on. We're getting out of here."

"What?" Sarah June struggled. "What do you mean? Where are we going?"

"To Kennicut, even if we have to walk across the bridge. Bonanza is too dangerous for us. Newcombe and Simmons have riled up everyone and anything that moves is likely to get ventilated." Emphasizing his point, a shotgun blast ripped a two-foot-wide hole in the tent. Lead shot spanged off one whiskey bottle and broke another.

"No!"

"What do you mean?" Slocum asked, more astounded than angry at the woman. "There's nothing to be gained staying here, and we can both lose our lives."

"I can't go until . . ." Sarah June's voice trailed off.

"We have to find somewhere safer than the Tons o'

Gold," Slocum said. He heard a raucous cry go up out in the street followed by the sounds of hand-to-hand fighting. Newcombe had sent his men down Bonanza's main street in an attempt to destroy the colonel's steam engine. Anyone caught in that brawl was certain to lose a few body parts.

"I'm not going, John. I can't."

"Why the hell not?"

"I was doing good here," she started.

"And the place is gone. Bonanza is gone, thanks to a pair of crazy rich men squabbling over a damned coffin!"

Sarah June looked at him. Her brown eyes welled with tears and then her lips thinned as resolve hardened.

"I don't care why they are fighting. I can't go until I make sure Lars and Bill are safe."

"Who're they? Other employees? Where's Abel?" Slocum wanted out of town, but saw Sarah June was not going to hurry her explanation. He settled back on his heels, drew his Colt Navy, and waited to see if anyone entered the Tons o' Gold.

"Abel's fine, I am sure," Sarah June said. "He lit out at the first shot. No, Lars and Bill are two miners. I was doing so well I thought I'd grubstake some prospectors. I gave them five hundred dollars."

"You can make more—if you're alive," Slocum said.

"It's not that. They hit it big, John. A huge silver strike, but Malcolm Newcombe heard about it before I did. They didn't even have time to tell me where their mine is. Newcombe kidnapped them and is trying to make me sell out the saloon."

"So give it to him."

"He knows Bill and Lars hit it big. Really rich. It'll assay out at fifteen ounces a ton. There's nothing close to it that's been found yet. Newcombe wants the Tons o'

Gold, but he wants their strike more. He took them prisoner."

"Newcombe or Eachin?"

"There's no difference between those snakes," Sarah June said bitterly. "Whatever Newcombe wants, Eachin delivers."

"Where are the miners being held?"

"I don't know for sure, but it's down the road, deeper in the canyon. You have to pass the blockhouse guarding the mouth of the toll road and then—" Sarah June shrugged, showing she had no idea where the two captive miners were being held.

"Eachin might have killed them outright," Slocum said, thinking aloud.

"He wouldn't, unless they signed over the claim to their mine. And even that wouldn't do. I'm majority owner because I grubstaked them, even if I don't know where the mine is."

"So Newcombe will want you, too," Slocum said, shaking his head in disgust. The more he tried to get away, the deeper the hole he'd dug for himself got. Sarah June wouldn't leave without knowing the fate of her two partners, and Malcolm Newcombe wanted her to sign over her rights so he could jump what might be the richest claim in the entire Bonanza strike. Colonel Simmons bringing in the railroad from Kennicut now changed everything in Bonanza.

If Malcolm Newcombe didn't strike fast and hard to gain control, the Kennicut sheriff and a big posse could reach the town inside an hour on the Colorado Grand Mountain Railroad.

Slocum didn't know if the lawman was inclined to do so, but it didn't matter. Newcombe still felt the need to assert his control now because Simmons could bring in his men.

Both wanted the wealth flowing from Bonanza—and both wanted the fancy coffin.

"John, will you help me? Please?"

Slocum looked into Sarah June's big brown eyes and knew he wasn't going to say no.

"Get somewhere safe," he told her. "Do you think Abel knows a bolt-hole to crawl into? Follow him." He looked at her for a moment, then kissed her. Sarah June seemed to melt in his arms, her body flowing against his.

"Good luck, John," she said softly. "I'll be waiting."

Slocum pushed her back and wondered if he was going to be lucky enough to return with her two grubstaked miners. For that, he wondered if he was going to return. The sound of battle raged outside, warning him neither side was going to let the matter drop until the other side was dead.

He left the Tons o' Gold and hunted for a mount until he found a frightened horse neighing and bucking at the sound of gunfire. Quieting the horse took a few minutes, and then Slocum was mounted and ready to ride. A small fire had started at the far end of town, possibly taking out the hotel and assay office. With the wan heat from the fire at his back, Slocum rode fast for the gate to the toll road.

The gate was open, but Slocum did not gallop through. He reined back and studied the blockhouse to the side of the road. It appeared to be deserted, as if all Newcombe's men had rushed into Bonanza for the big fight. Slocum knew better than to risk his neck making such an assumption. One guard with a rifle could pick him off if he got too careless.

Slocum snorted in disgust, thinking what he was doing. He had no idea if Eachin held the miners prisoner or if he had killed them outright. With them dead—and Sarah June to follow—who was to dispute any claim Newcombe had to the land around Bonanza? The assay office held what deeds there were, and it was going up in flames. If Newcombe never learned the location of Sarah June's fabulous strike, it hardly mattered.

He knew the silver was somewhere in the mountains and would have ownership of all the land.

Slocum considered another possibility. Eachin might never have told his boss about Sarah June's involvement and might be angling to steal the claim for himself.

Not knowing what he rode into made Slocum edgy, but he rode up to the gate and waited for any sign of a guard. When no one showed, Slocum drew his six-shooter, cocked it, and then called out.

"Whatcha want?" came a drunk voice from the blockhouse. A man poked his head up over the edge and rested a rifle next to him.

Slocum aimed and fired in one smooth motion. The man's head vanished, and as he did slurred demands to know who was at the gate. Slocum waited another minute to flush more guards. Only when silence greeted him did he ride through the gate and go to the guardhouse. He tethered his horse and ducked inside, not sure what he was hunting for.

A slow smile crossed his face when he saw a large map pinned to one wall showing the entire length of the toll road. Several spots just off the road were marked with smeary black Xs. One had a red X.

"Where would Malcolm Newcombe most likely be holed up?" Slocum asked himself aloud. He laughed without humor. The black marks showed where guards could bunk down. The red X had to indicate something more important—like Newcombe's cabin.

Slocum quickly estimated the distance and got back on his horse, riding hard. Even if the miners weren't held at Newcombe's, taking the toll road owner hostage would help his cause. Slocum figured he could trade Malcolm Newcombe for the pair, and if Eachin had already killed his prisoners, Newcombe could go to Kennicut to stand trial.

He sobered thinking that he needed Colonel Simmons's railroad to get Newcombe across Knife Canyon. He doubted Simmons would ever turn his rival over to the law. A trade of freedom for the coffin seemed more likely.

Slocum hunkered down as he rode. He had to do it all himself and not rely on the law or the colonel. He came upon a well-traveled side road before he knew it and took it without hesitation. Supply wagons cut the deep ruts into the road. Even if this didn't go to Newcombe's cabin, it led somewhere important.

A quarter mile off the road Slocum saw a veritable mansion. He had expected Newcombe to live better than his guards but not like this. Most of the take from the toll road had gone into building a fabulous mansion rivaling anything he had ever seen along State Street in Denver.

The house appeared as deserted as the toll road, save for an outbuilding where a pale yellow light shone through a window. Slocum left that for later and rode boldly to the front of the house. He tied up his horse and went in the front door and looked around. The darkness held no secrets worth revealing, he decided. The silence was complete.

Slocum passed through the hallway and into the kitchen, going out to the back porch where he could watch the outbuilding. Four horses were tethered beside the small shack. If Bill and Lars rode with Eachin, that meant Newcombe's henchman had an accomplice. Slocum knew there might be more, their horses in the distant barn.

On cat's feet, he crossed the yard and peered in the window. Two men sat back to back, hands bound and nooses around both their necks. The middle of the rope had been tossed over a beam. If either moved, he would strangle not only himself but his partner. Slocum hunted in the dark corners of the room for sign of Eachin and his cohort. A dark form covered with a blanket lay stretched on a bunk. But where was the second man?

Slocum went to the door and carefully opened it, wary of any betraying squeaks from unoiled hinges. He got inside without alerting the sleeping man, although one of the miners saw him and started to cry out. Slocum put his finger to his lips, silencing the man. Slocum pointed to the sleeper, then shrugged his shoulders in a silent plea for help. Bill and Lars had to know if there were other guards.

Since neither spoke, Slocum reckoned another guard was nearby. He went to the sleeping man and pulled back the blanket.

"Hello, Eachin," Slocum said nastily, sticking his six-shooter into the man's face.

The frightened expression was almost reward enough for all Eachin had done to him. But not quite.

"Move and I'll blow a hole in your worthless head," Slocum said. Louder, he called to the bound men, "Where's the other guard?"

"Comin' in the door! Behind you!" shouted the miner facing the door.

Slocum snarled, spun and fired as the startled guard dropped an armload of wood and went for his six-gun. Slocum's slug hit the man squarely in the chest and drove him back outside, where he flopped onto his back. He kicked feebly and then even this small sign of life faded away.

But the brief, deadly gunfight gave Eachin the chance he needed. He swung around on the bed and kicked like a mule. Slocum stumbled forward, tripped, and went to his knees. He hit the floor hard but didn't stay down.

Slocum rolled so he could bring his Colt to bear on Eachin. The only problem was that Eachin hadn't stayed put.

"He's goin' fer his gun," the miner facing away from the door warned.

Slocum frantically sought Eachin. By the time he spotted him in the far corner of the room, Eachin had his gun out. Slocum had to shoot past the bound miners—but he did. He had to, if he wanted to stay alive.

Two shots rang out as one. Slocum winced but felt only wood splinters from the floor cutting his arm. Eachin's bullet had come close, but not close enough. Slocum's had found a good target in the man's leg.

Eachin cursed and sprayed lead all over the room. Slocum was forced to roll, reverse direction, and tried to get to his feet because the two prisoners provided Eachin with a living shield. Before Slocum could get Newcombe's henchman in his sights again, Eachin dived through the window amid shattering glass and loud cries of pain.

"Git that varmint. Don't let 'im get away!" shouted one miner.

Slocum had no intention of letting Eachin get away, but that's what happened. By the time he got to the door, Eachin had pulled himself onto a horse and was riding off at top speed. Slocum fired twice at the retreating gunman, but knew neither shot hit his target.

"Kin you git this here noose off our necks?" asked the miner facing the door. "I'm parched and my neck's stretched and—"

"Don't move," Slocum said. He picked up a hatchet and swung it once. The sharp blade parted the strands of the rope and let the miners tumble away from each other. It took him only two more slices to get their hands free, but neither man was able to stand for several minutes.

"Go on after 'im," one miner said.

"Are you Bill or Lars?" asked Slocum.

"Why, you know us!" The miner awkwardly slapped his partner on the shoulder and then winced. "Miss Daniels sent you, I reckon. I'm Bill Parsons and this here no-account is my partner, Lars Dorch."

Slocum helped them to their feet. Circulation returned slowly to their legs and hands, and by they time they got outside Slocum knew Eachin was long gone. Wounded, he would be even more dangerous, if that were possible.

"Get on those horses."

"They ain't ours," Lars said worrying over legalities. "It'd be horse stealin' to take 'em."

"Newcombe owes you. Eachin owes you. We'll argue later, after we're out of this canyon." Slocum looked up at the towering, steep black walls and shivered. They were still in enemy territory, and Eachin would round up any guard left along the toll road to come after them.

Speed was their only chance, and Slocum saw from the painful progress the two miners made, that they were in no shape to make haste.

"You boys follow close," Slocum told them. "I'll try to flush out any trouble. If you hear gunshots, get off the road, circle around and try to get the hell out of the canyon while I'm taking care of business."

"You don't have to tell us that twice, mister," Lars declared.

Slocum studied them to be sure both men would not fall from the saddle, then got his horse and trotted back in the direction of the gate leading off the toll road. The occasional stands of trees around made him uneasy. He imagined Eachin lurking in every inky patch. Occasionally Slocum turned and looked behind him to be sure the miners were still following.

The closer they got to the gate, the more keyed up Slocum got. There had been no choice about exit from the canyon and Eachin had to know that. Slocum hoped the man had been so badly injured that he had crawled off into the bushes to die, but he wasn't counting on it.

Slocum reined back when he was within a hundred yards of the gate and waited for Bill and Lars to catch up. He had stayed alive trusting his sixth sense and it was screaming for him to be cautious now.

"What's the problem?" asked Bill. "There's the gate. We kin make it in a couple minutes."

"Eachin is out there," Slocum said. He turned slowly, studying the darkness. One area looked like another, but he stared hard into an impenetrable spot near the block-house. Slocum could not have told why. It just seemed the most likely place for a sniper.

"Where's the varmint?" asked Lars. "I'll rip his throat out 'n—"

"Quiet," snapped Slocum. "Do either of you have a gun?" He bent over and looked to answer his own question. If either man had carried a rifle, it was long gone. He had his six-shooter and the rifle in the saddle holster. The former owner of the horse had not maintained the rifle well. It hadn't been oiled for months, and Slocum was not going to waste time checking how many cartridges were in the magazine. He had to trust to luck.

"Listen close. I'll draw fire, probably from over by the blockhouse. You both hightail it through the gate while I'm pinning down the gunman."

"Where's the shooter?" asked Bill, squinting.

"Let him be," said Lars, punching his partner's shoulder. "He ain't done wrong by us yet. We're ready. Both of us."

Slocum nodded, levered a round into the rifle chamber and put his heels to the horse's flanks. With a loud rebel yell, he galloped straight for the blockhouse. Before he had ridden twenty yards he saw he was right.

Lances of flame lashed forth, showing the location of the hidden sniper. The flare of one shot cast a vivid light on the face of the marksman.

Roy Eachin.

Slocum yelled again and began firing as he rode, hoping the two miners followed his orders and got through the gate while he went after Eachin.

17

Slocum kept his head down as he galloped straight down Eachin's barrel. He jerked as a bullet tore his sleeve and left a bloody crease, but he never slowed. When he got closer to where Eachin crouched, he fired as fast as he could jack shells into the chamber. When the rifle seized up, Slocum dropped it without an instant's regret and drew his six-shooter.

He had only three shots left, but he used them all. Then his horse vaulted over Eachin and pounded away behind the blockhouse. Slocum glanced back and saw Eachin painfully moving to swing his rifle around. Slocum had wounded the man a second time but had failed once more to get in a killing shot.

Then Slocum rode out of range. He cut through a few straggly pines and reined in to let his lathered horse catch its breath. A few yards away rose the barbed wire fence. When the horse felt ready, Slocum started toward the fence. The horse had jumped it once. It could do it again, although the fence was much taller than Eachin had been. As Slocum felt the horse begin its leap, a shot rang out.

The horse shuddered in midair and then hit the ground

on the far side of the fence. It took a few more strides and then collapsed under Slocum. He hit the ground hard and lay stunned for a moment. The sound of Eachin cursing a blue streak got Slocum moving. He was out of ammo, his horse was dead, and Eachin was fighting like a cornered rat.

Slocum hated doing it, but he scrambled for the bushes a few yards away and hid while Eachin roved back and forth, hunting for his quarry.

"Come out. Slocum! Come out so I can kill you! You mangy son of a bitch!" Eachin raged but Slocum did not rise to the challenge. He laid still and watched Eachin, wishing he had one last round in his trusty Colt. That would end this here and now, but Slocum was out of ammo.

Seething at his inability to do anything, Slocum watched from cover until Eachin stalked off. From the way the man walked, both of Slocum's rounds had caught him in the same leg. Only when Eachin vanished did Slocum retreat, slipping into the night and beginning the long walk into Bonanza.

He sucked in his breath when he saw the road back was brightly lit by the towers of sparks caused as the town went up in flames.

Heat on his face, Slocum skirted the worst of the blaze and headed for the far end of town where the Tons o' Gold still stood. He blinked when he saw the light inside shining through dozens of bullet holes. It was as if a giant moth had devoured large hunks of the canvas and then moved on. His hand rested on the ebony butt of his six-gun, but he knew he had to find other ways of fighting if it came to that. No ammo. The words echoed in his head until it threatened to deafen him.

Pulling back the flap, he chanced a quick glance inside. The saloon was deserted except for Sarah June Daniels.

She sat at a beer-stained table in the middle of the tent, a half-filled bottle of whiskey in front of her. She knocked back a shot as he slipped into the tent.

"Drinking alone isn't a good sign," Slocum said. Sarah June jumped. She had not seen him.

"John! You made it! Bill and Lars thought Eachin had killed you!" She jumped to her feet and ran to him. She threw her arms around him and hugged so tightly he gasped for breath. He felt her hot tears soaking into his shirt as she sobbed.

"I'm harder to get rid of than that fire burning the town to the ground," he said.

Sarah June sniffed and wiped at her eyes. She smiled almost shyly. "I should have known Eachin couldn't stop you."

"Did the miners make it in one piece?" Slocum asked.

"Yes, Bill and Lars are fine as frog's fur," she said, still sniffing. She looked up at him with an expression he could not fathom. "I thought I'd lost you," she said in a small voice.

Then Sarah June clung to him and sobbed even harder.

"Bonanza can be rebuilt," he told her, "and the Tons o' Gold seems in pretty good shape."

"To hell with that," she said fiercely. Sarah June lifted her face to him, closed her eyes, and waited. Slocum shared her need. He kissed her with a passion that signaled desire as hot as the fire burning through the town.

Slocum pulled her close and felt her full, firm breasts crush into his chest. Her lips were headier than any liquor served in the saloon and Slocum drank his fill. When his lips parted slightly he felt Sarah June's quick, agile, pink tongue slip into his mouth and play hide and seek. Their tongues dueled amorously, rolling over and over, stroking and caressing and promising both even more.

"Oh, John," she gasped, pulling back slightly. "I need you. I need you now!"

He answered with actions, not words. His lips kissed her cheek and eyelids and forehead, and then he worked on one shell-like ear. His tongue dipped in slightly before he began nibbling on her tender earlobe. He felt Sarah June sag in his arms. Her legs turned weak from the rush of passion coursing throughout her trim body.

She threw her arms around his neck to support herself, but Slocum ducked down so he could kiss her jaw and work underneath, to the brunette's throat—and lower. One by one the buttons on her blouse popped open to reveal the surge of her proud breasts. Slocum licked and kissed first one meaty slope and then the other.

"Here, let me help," she said. Sarah June shrugged off her blouse and stood before him naked to the waist. Slocum pounced on one cherry-capped summit and drew the tip into his mouth, caressing it with his lips. Then he sucked. Hard.

This robbed Sarah June of all strength. She sank down, forcing him to grab her and lift. He spun about and deposited her on the edge of the table where she had been drinking. Groping, he tried to sweep away the bottle but Sarah June caught his wrist.

"Wait," she said. The sultry brunette lifted the half-filled bottle and poured the liquor over her breasts. "Go on. Enjoy."

"I will, with or without the booze," he said. He lapped and licked at the succulent mounds, now turned headier than ever with the addition of the alcoholic rinse.

Sarah June sank to the table, supporting herself on her elbows. Every time Slocum's tongue raked over a sensitive nubbin atop one breast or the other, a tremor passed through her body. Without even realizing it, her legs parted in wanton invitation.

"More, John, give me more," she gasped out. She struggled to hike up her skirts and expose her most private parts.

"Let me," he said, taking the bottle from her trembling hand. He poured a little of the liquor over her nether lips, then dived down to suck and lick and tongue those pink, scalloped flaps. When his tongue drove fast into her most intimate recess, Sarah June let out a loud cry of release. Her entire body shook like a leaf in a high wind. She thrashed about on the table, held captive by his tongue.

And then she grated out, "More, damn you. I want more of you!"

Slocum licked a few times on her soft, white inner thighs and then worked his way up to the dome of her heaving belly. He wanted her to be ready—more than ready—when he entered her the next time.

Sarah June was sobbing and moaning with stark pleasure by the time Slocum stood and unfastened his gun belt. He kicked it aside and began working on the buttons on his jeans.

"Wait, no," Sarah June said.

"You've changed your mind?" The idea hit Slocum like an avalanche.

"I want to do it," she said, the impish smile dancing on her lips again. She sat up and ran her fingers over his rock-hard belly and then moved lower to his equally rock-hard manhood. Sarah June popped the buttons fast and drew out his stalk, circling it in her hand. She moved up and down slowly, tormenting him. Slocum felt as if his guts had turned to liquid fire.

"I want—"

"No," she said, grabbing his wrist. "Let me get you started, really started. You'll enjoy this." Sarah June bent over and caught only the purpled tip of his shaft in her lips. Her tongue swirled about like a miniature tornado, sweeping away his control. Slocum gulped and fought to keep from acting like a young buck with his first woman. Sarah June's mouth was educated and knew all the right places to brush, to press, to fleetingly torment with her tongue and lips and teeth.

When Slocum couldn't stand it any longer, he pushed her back flat on the table and moved into the bushy delta spread before him.

"Go on, John, go—oh! Ohh!" Sarah June shivered again, as if she had caught a cold. But the hot flush rising on her breasts and flooding upward told Slocum it was something else. He sank into her depths and felt her clamp down firmly around him. Then her entire body exploded again.

He braced himself, hands on either side of her hips. As her climax died, he began a steady stroking motion. He sank all the way into her heated depths, then pulled out at the same speed. She was warm and moist and clinging all around him. Slocum stared down at her breasts bobbing about with every thrust he made and got even harder at the sight.

He reached out and tweaked her nipples but found he could not stroke the way he wanted, the way he needed. His hands slipped down her smooth sides and then cupped her buttocks. When he rammed forward the next time, he lifted with both hands. Her rump felt like dough waiting to be kneaded. He squeezed down hard and was rewarded with delightful new pressure all around his hidden length.

"John, John, you fill me up. You're so big. You're like a stallion!"

He robbed her of coherent speech by picking up the tempo of his movement. He thought of a piston on a steam engine, starting slowly and then building up steam. It was the same with him except he lost control along the way. He felt the white-hot tide rising within his loins and knew he had only seconds more of this extreme pleasure.

Slocum crushed the double handful of flesh he held at the same time Sarah June tensed all over. She slammed down hard on his manhood and milked him delightfully. He pumped in and out the best he could and then the winds of desire blowing through him died. Slocum took a half step back and looked down at the woman still spread wide before him.

The sight was almost enough to get him hard again. Almost.

Through lust-heavy lids, the brunette stared up at him.

"I knew you were worth waiting for," Sarah June told him.

"I'm glad I came back for my reward."

"Reward?" she said, grinning. "That wasn't your reward. The best is yet to come!"

Slocum started to claim his reward but stopped. Something had changed. For a moment he could not identify the problem. Then he realized the fighting outside had stopped. He hesitated about tending to Sarah June again, but the woman settled the matter. She noticed the lack of gunfire, too.

"Do you think they've killed everyone off?" she asked in a small voice. She pushed down her skirts and began buttoning her blouse. "I've got to see."

Slocum pulled up his pants and got his gun belt settled around his waist, aware that the six-shooter was for show only until he reloaded. He needed to get back to the train and the freight car his gear was stowed in, and not for the first time since riding in style over Knife Canyon on the fancy train, he wished he had his mare, still stabled in Kennicut.

"The fires have died down," Sarah June said, peeking through the tent flap. Slocum was bolder and threw the flap open wide so he could see what was happening.

Or not happening. Bonanza was as silent as a grave now.

"They might be regrouping," Slocum said. "There's only so much town to burn to the ground, and even Newcombe needs time to regroup his men."

"Look yonder, John," Sarah June said. She pointed in the direction of the unfinished railroad depot the colonel had thrown up to service Bonanza. Men moved about aimlessly, but there seemed to be no hostilities. "Do you think the colonel won?"

"Even if he lost, I reckon we can count on him for an hour long speech telling how he came out on top."

"I hope Bill and Lars are all right," Sarah June said. She looked at him in disgust when she saw his expression. "It's not like that. They are going to make me rich, not get me excited."

"Can't tell much difference when silver bullion is dangled in front of you," Slocum said.

"Oh, you!" Sarah June playfully punched his arm. "They're miners, nothing more. I like them and don't want them hurt, but I do own fifty-one percent of their mine."

"Do you know where it is?"

"They stopped by after you rescued them but didn't tell me. Not exactly," she said with some hesitation. "I know they wouldn't cheat me."

Slocum ignored the obvious. For enough money, any man would cheat.

"I'll see what the colonel has to say."

"And see how his redheaded daughter is getting along?" Sarah June accused.

"Why not? She still owes me," Slocum said. He waited for Sarah June to bristle, then added, "She still owes me a month's salary. That's all. And we're not even friends."

Slocum made his way down Bonanza's littered street

to the depot, hardly more than a shack with a platform. Beyond it were two sidings for moving freight cars and turning around the engine. Otherwise, the Colorado Grand Mountain Railroad showed little presence in Bonanza.

Yet.

"What's going on?" Slocum asked a miner who was leaning on a bloodied ax handle. The man swung the ash rod around and squared off as if he intended to block Slocum's way. The miner gave him a once over and relaxed.

"You ain't with Newcombe, are you?"

"The only way I'd be with that son of a bitch would be to shoot him," Slocum said, resting his hand on the butt of his Colt Navy. This was the password needed to get past the miner.

"Not if I get to him first," the man said with rancor.

"Is the colonel fixing on returning to Kennicut for more men?" Slocum asked, noting the activity at the rear car on Simmons's train.

"Don't rightly know what he's intendin' to do. Whatever it is, I'm with 'im. Him and his boys saved my hide. Two of Newcombe's men was whupin' up on me. I wasn't the only one they saved, either."

Slocum had no stomach to listen to the stories of the fight. He moved closer and spotted Rebecca. He waved to her, but the redhead did not see him. With a twist and turn, he forced his way through the crowd and reached the rear of the train in time to see O'Brien and three other men unloading the fancy coffin Simmons had bought to replace the one stolen by Malcolm Newcombe.

"O'Brien!" Slocum called. "What're you doing?"

"The colonel's driven Newcombe's men back to the toll road," O'Brien said. "He told me to fetch this casket and take it to the gate."

"Why?"

Slocum saw the expression on O'Brien's face and knew the engineer had not bothered asking. He simply followed orders.

"Where's Rebecca?"

"She was here a minute ago." O'Brien looked around and almost dropped his corner of the coffin. The others grunted in disapproval and O'Brien gave up hunting for the woman.

"You want some company?" Slocum asked. "I'll come along, but I need to get some more ammo."

"Hurry it up. We'll be on our way to the toll road gate," O'Brien said.

Slocum spent a few more minutes looking for Rebecca but did not find her. He jumped into the freight car where all the crew's personal effects had been stored. It took him ten minutes to find his saddlebags and reload. He felt better knowing he could cut down Eachin—or Malcolm Newcombe—if he got them in his sights.

He returned to the Tons o' Gold Saloon but Sarah June had left, probably to track down the two miners. He had put a bug in her ear about the location of their fabulous silver strike. As principal shareholder, she deserved to know where the mother lode was. Slocum swung onto the horse he had stolen, then trotted out of Bonanza and down the hill back to the gate.

Slocum had left it virtually deserted. Eachin might be on guard or in the blockhouse tending his wounds. Wherever the man was, a dozen or more of Newcombe's other guards were in position for a real fight.

"You're not coming onto the toll road, Colonel," barked Malcolm Newcombe from the top of the blockhouse. He stood so only the top of his head poked up. Slocum knew he could take off the man's head with a well placed rifle shot, but Colonel Simmons didn't look as if he was interested in that.

The colonel rode nervously back and forth in front of the gate, his hands fluttering like pale bats and his jitters being picked up by the men behind him.

"I don't want your damned toll road, Newcombe!" the colonel shouted. "I want to swap. I have a fancy new coffin. I'll trade it for the one you stole from me!"

Slocum sagged when he realized these two still played their silly game using men's lives as pawns. Bonanza was burned to the ground, and the number left dead wouldn't be known for days. The mountains above Bonanza were filled with riches enough for everyone, and yet the two argued over a coffin.

"Why?" shouted back Newcombe. "I like the one I got. Keep that one. You'll be needing it soon, Simmons!"

Slocum knew the tone of voice and shouted, "Down! Everyone hit the ground!"

His warning was drowned out in a barrage coming from the other side of the barbed wire fence. A half dozen of Simmons's crew and a few miners went down under the cowardly attack.

"Forward!" screeched Simmons. "Attack them! Kill them!"

Slocum watched as Simmons led the charge against Newcombe's fortified position. It quickly became a senseless, bloody slaughter.

18

"O'Brien!" Slocum shouted. "Go back! Get your men back or they'll be shot!" His words were drowned out by a new fusillade from the top of the blockhouse beside the toll road. The miners and railroad men with Simmons rallied for a moment and returned fire, shouting bravely as they charged, but another hail of lead cut down even more of their number. Any sane commander would order his men to retreat and regroup after taking such devastating casualties, but Simmons was still at the gate, shrieking for a renewed attack.

Slocum had always marveled at how God protected drunks and the insane. If this was true, Simmons rode safely in God's hip pocket. Men all around him died or were wounded seriously, but not a single slug found its way to end his miserable life.

O'Brien dropped the coffin he and the other three from the railroad crew carried and signaled an immediate withdrawal for those men still standing. It didn't take much coaxing for the crew with him to get the hell out of range of Newcombe's snipers. As they crept back to a more defensible, safer position, the miners noticed they were alone with the crazy colonel and began to zigzag their way out of range, too.

"Give it to me!" cried Colonel Simmons, waving his fist in Newcombe's direction. "I want you to give me my coffin!"

"I'll see you in hell before I give it back!" shouted Newcombe, waving his fist in response. The two men tried to out-shout one another until the conclusion became apparent to everyone in earshot, even to the participants.

Slocum saw that Simmons was not going to give up, and neither was Malcolm Newcombe. After shouting themselves hoarse, the two fell silent. Then the crazed railroad magnate yanked his horse about and trotted for cover amid the bullets trying to find a target in his back. Again he seemed to live a blessed life. All Newcombe's riflemen missed.

The fight was taking on the air of a Mexican standoff. Slocum got an idea of how to end the fight in a hurry and to satisfy his own need for revenge. He dropped from horseback and ran to the fence while Newcombe's men were firing at Colonel Simmons. Slocum flopped belly down in the soft dirt and wriggled under the sharp, lower strand of barbed wire, rolled when he reached the other side, and found cover behind low-growing bushes a few yards inside.

He waited to be sure no one had spotted him, then he went hunting for Roy Eachin. Slocum doubted Newcombe's right-hand man was far off, not with two of Slocum's bullets in his leg. Bent over, Slocum flitted from one patch of cover to the next, getting closer and closer to the blockhouse. Slocum approached it from the canyon side while all the snipers inside were busy hunting for targets among Simmons's men on the other side of the gate.

Slocum chanced a quick look through the narrow doorway. A half-dozen men sat at a table strewn with cartridges, reloading rifles for those upstairs. He didn't see Eachin. Slocum pressed his back against the outside wall when he heard someone on the catwalk above his head. Looking straight up at the starry sky along the palisade, he saw Malcolm Newcombe peering into the darkness cloaking the toll road.

Colt Navy aimed squarely on the toll road magnate's head, Slocum held off firing at the easy target. Newcombe hunted for something. What did he hope to see back along the road? Reinforcements from the other end of the toll road?

"Where *is* that good-for-nothing?" Newcombe grumbled, then vanished. Slocum had no idea who Newcombe meant.

He turned his attention back to the men inside the blockhouse, hoping to catch a glimpse of Eachin. Where was Newcombe's right-hand man? Slocum saw a row of bunks, but no one rested on them. If Eachin was here, he would be laid up. Or would he be up on the catwalk directing the attack against Colonel Simmons?

Slocum pulled up his bandanna so that it partially shielded his face, then boldly walked into the room. Only one of the men reloading the rifles looked up.

"Hey, you!"

"What?" Slocum growled, not turning as he made his way to the ladder leading up to the roof.

"Make yourself useful and take some of these with you." The man pointed to a half-dozen rifles waiting to be carried to the men above.

Slocum grunted, nodded and kept his face down. He didn't know if any of the men would recognize him, especially since Murdoch had been killed trying to blow up the bridge across Knife Canyon, but Slocum wasn't taking any chances on this score. He scooped up the rifles and clumsily climbed the ladder to the fortified roof. Palisades protected the men from the neck down and a catwalk afforded a higher position from which to fire if the snipers knelt.

Slocum dumped the rifles in a stack in the middle of the roof, keeping one for himself. It was darker here, and he prowled about with impunity. Newcombe shouted curses over the top of the wall at Simmons and the rest of his guards had their attention focused out, not behind them.

Eachin was nowhere to be seen. Slocum considered ending the fight by taking Malcolm Newcombe prisoner. All he need do was walk up, draw his six-shooter, and stuff it into the man's ear. As tempting as the plan was, Slocum saw that Newcombe was as fanatical as Colonel Simmons. The toll road owner was likely to prefer death to surrendering the coffin.

Slocum lived by odds when he gambled. This was not a gamble that favored him.

"Where's Eachin?" he asked one guard at the wall. The man half-turned and Slocum shoved his loaded rifle at the man while yanking the guard's from his grip.

"Eachin's with the coffin. Where else do you suppose he'd be?"

"Down the road?" Slocum asked.

"Yeah, of course." The man's hat flew off as a stray bullet came winging from the direction of Colonel Simmons's line. Furious, the man took the rifle Slocum had just handed him and emptied it. Without a word, Slocum handed him back his original rifle and dropped the empty one on the pile. Slocum grabbed another loaded rifle and headed to the trapdoor leading to the room below.

He skinned down the ladder and walked out before any of the men at the table could ask where he was going. Slocum heaved a sigh of relief. He had walked into the enemy's den and had emerged unscathed. Rifle clutched in his hands, he set off down the toll road in search of Eachin.

After less than ten minutes' walking, Slocum saw a dark shape in the middle of the road. He left the road and circled, coming up from the side on a wagon parked in the road. A tarp covered what could only be Colonel Simmons's precious casket. But Slocum didn't see a guard anywhere.

No Eachin. Nobody.

He scouted the wagon and made sure it was deserted. Only then did Slocum crawl on hands and knees hunting for tracks in the dark to tell him where Eachin might have gone. He found boot imprints heading off into the trees in the soft dirt alongside the road. Why Eachin had left the coffin unguarded puzzled Slocum, but he intended to be cautious as he followed the trail into the stand of pines mixed in with a few piñons.

His nose wrinkled and gave him warning before he saw Eachin. Eachin had gone into the woods to relieve himself. Killing the man with his pants down might have provided a justified end to the backshooter's foul life, but Slocum wasn't up to it.

"Eachin?" he said softly. "You here?"

"Who's there? 'Course I'm here. Where'd you think I would go?"

"See any bears?" Slocum asked, enjoying the byplay with the irritated man.

"Let me cover up my pile," Eachin said irritably. "Does Newcombe want his damned box now?"

"Reckon so," Slocum said, slipping away. He still held the rifle but thought his six-gun might be a better weapon in the forested area.

He heard Eachin grunt and then scrabble in the soft dirt to cover his scat. Newcombe's henchman came from the woods, muttering to himself. When he stepped away from the tree closest to the road, he stopped and looked around.

"Where'd you get off to?" he called. "Who the hell are you?"

"Your worst nightmare," Slocum said in the same soft voice he had used in the woods. He came up behind Eachin, the rifle aimed at the man's spine. The lightest tug on the trigger would end the man's miserable life once and for all. "Your leg hurt where I shot you?"

"Slocum!"

Eachin ducked and started to spin as he went for his six-shooter. His game leg saved his life. His right leg gave way under the quick turn and threw him to the ground at the same instant Slocum fired. His rifle bullet whined past Eachin and embedded in the wood side of the wagon.

"Die, Slocum! You miserable mongrel!" Eachin flopped around on the ground and got the butt of his six-gun steadied so he could shoot. The first round went wide. The second came close enough to make Slocum jerk away involuntarily. This spoiled his second shot.

Slocum feinted to the right and dodged left, taking refuge behind a rough-barked spruce tree. A bullet tore a hunk off the trunk, keeping Slocum behind it for a moment. When he chanced a quick peek around, Eachin had vanished.

Guessing where the wounded man would go, Slocum cocked his six-shooter and aimed at the wagon—and waited. During the war he had been a sniper and a good one. He sometimes would sit all day on a hill waiting for the flash of sunlight off a Union officer's gold braid. A single shot could turn the course of a battle and often had, thanks to Slocum's patience and accuracy.

As had happened before, Slocum out-waited his adversary. Eachin got antsy and rose in the bed of the wagon, silhouetted darkly against the far wall of the canyon. Slocum's finger came back in a slow, smooth motion. His six-gun bucked, and Eachin tumbled backward with a loud clatter.

Slocum felt good about the shot but cautiously approached the wagon and looked in the bed. Sprawled over Colonel Simmons's coffin lay Eachin. His six-shooter had fallen from his lifeless hand, and his head canted at a strange angle. Hopping into the wagon, Slocum poked the man with the barrel of his pistol. Nothing.

Looking closer, Slocum saw his shot had caught Eachin in the forehead and had snapped his head around.

"Good riddance," Slocum said, holstering his Colt Navy and grabbing the front of Eachin's shirt. He heaved and dumped the man over the side of the wagon. Slocum had settled the debt he owed for all Eachin had done to Rebecca and had tried to do to Sarah June, but he still felt strangely unsatisfied. Kneeling, he put his hand on the cool surface of the fancy coffin.

There was still work to be done.

Clambering into the driver's seat, Slocum caught up the reins and got the team pulling grudgingly in the direction of the gate where the fight still raged. He wasn't sure he could do it but thought he might be able to drive pell-mell through the gate and deliver the casket to the colonel without getting too shot up. Surprise and speed were his only allies since he was likely to draw fire from both sides.

But it would bring the senseless war to an end. That was worth the risk since so many had already died.

Slocum had driven the wagon only fifty yards when he heard horses approaching from the direction of New-combe's blockhouse. He touched the six-shooter in its holster and knew he could never shoot it out with a half-dozen men. From the thundering sound of the hooves, he would soon face at least that many.

Cursing under his breath, Slocum brought the team to a halt, fastened the reins around the brake, and then jumped from the box. He barely had time to fling himself prone in a shallow drainage ditch alongside the road when the riders reached the wagon.

"Where's Eachin?" demanded the lead rider.

"How the hell should I know? We was all back at the gate takin' potshots at the colonel's men."

"Like crows on a fence, they was," another chimed in, laughing. "I want to get back and finish the chore. I ain't had so much fun since we was in Denver and shot that peddler for sellin' us that bottle of snake oil."

"Shut yer pie hole," snapped the lead rider. "Eachin!" he shouted. "Where are you?"

"Might be he found something more fun to do than sittin' on a coffin."

"Might be he's in the coffin tryin' it out," the man who had killed the peddler said. Slocum watched them from a few yards away. It took a measure of willpower not to answer the man, letting him know what had happened to Eachin.

"Shut up," the leader repeated. "Caleb, get your butt into the wagon and drive it to the gate for Mr. Newcombe."

A rider at the back of the pack jumped from horseback into the wagon and expertly took the reins. The team complained a mite and then began pulling the wagon and its cargo toward the gate, where Newcombe held Simmons at bay.

Slocum got up and dusted himself off. He started hoofing it toward the gate, a thousand different schemes running through his head. He discarded them all as impractical or too dangerous, as if trying to drive the wagon with the coffin through the gate hadn't been both. Slocum neared the gate, again ignored because he came from along the toll road and all attention focused on the Bonanza side of the fence.

The wagon had been placed near the blockhouse. Slocum wondered what was going to happen when he saw Malcolm Newcombe come striding out as bold as brass. The owner of the toll road hopped into the wagon bed and then stood on the coffin.

"Simmons!" he shouted. "I've got your coffin. And it's all mine. You'll never get it back!" To the men in the guardhouse, Newcombe said in a lower voice, "Cut him down when he shows himself."

Slocum drew a bead on Newcombe's back, ready to take out the man if his guards shot the colonel. He owed nothing to Simmons or his daughter, but that didn't stop Slocum from feeling an obligation to fair play. He started to call out to Newcombe when he saw O'Brien approaching the gate waving a white flag.

If Newcombe did not honor the truce, he was a dead man. But the move seemed to confuse Newcombe.

"Hold on," Newcombe said, waving to his snipers. "That's not Simmons."

"I want to parley," O'Brien shouted. "Send out a man to negotiate for you, Newcombe!"

"Like hell. I'm no coward like the man you work for. I do my own talking!" Newcombe jumped to the ground and strutted out to the gate. He and O'Brien spent several minutes talking before the engineer turned and retreated, still under the truce flag.

Slocum edged closer to the wagon, looking for a chance to steal it. That would put an end to the conflict because he doubted Newcombe had the strange emotional attachment to it that the colonel did. All Newcombe wanted was to tweak the colonel's nose. For the railroad magnate the coffin meant far more.

"Give it to me," Newcombe said, reaching over and

whipping a guard's six-shooter from its holster. Before Slocum knew what was happening, Newcombe stalked back to the gate, unfastened the chain and went to the other side.

In spite of himself, Slocum stepped forward, then joined the rest of Newcombe's men at the gate. It took him a few seconds to figure out what was going on. He started to cry out, then held his tongue. Surrounded by Newcombe's men as he was, he had no chance to escape if he drew unwanted attention to himself.

Besides, Slocum wasn't sure this wasn't the proper way to end the dispute.

Colonel Simmons walked out slowly, a six-shooter in his hand. The two men eyed themselves like stags fighting for the leadership of a herd. They exchanged angry words, then stood back to back, raised their pistols to point skyward, and began counting out their paces.

"Wait, no, stop!" came the cry. Slocum blinked in surprise. Rebecca's frightened cry came from behind him, from somewhere along the toll road. He turned and saw the red-haired woman and Buster Newcombe riding up, waving their arms and both shouting for their fathers to stop their duel.

They raced through the gate, giving Slocum his chance. He quickly followed, along with a dozen of Newcombe's men.

But the duel was nearing its fatal conclusion. The two combatants had counted to ten, turned, and leveled their six-guns. Two shots rang out as one, filling the still night air with clouds of pungent, billowing white gunsmoke.

The pair stood for a moment, as if thinking about taking second shots. Then both Simmons and Newcombe sagged to the ground.

19

Rebecca ran to kneel beside her father. From the way she cradled the colonel's head in her lap, Slocum knew the railroad magnate was dead. He turned to see Buster Newcombe walk slowly to where his father kicked weakly. The younger Newcombe stared down at the dying man but did nothing to aid him. Shortly, even the feeble kicks faded. Buster Newcombe turned away, a blank look on his face.

"He's dead," Slocum said, checking Malcolm Newcombe to be sure.

"I reckon that's true," Buster said in a monotone. He looked to where Rebecca cried openly over her father's corpse. "It had to happen this way. They were too stubborn to ever give up."

"They killed each other because of coffins," Slocum said, struck by the irony of it. There were two coffins and two dead men. He wondered if the offspring of the two businessmen would fight over which of their fathers got planted in which box. From all that had gone on, Slocum did not doubt that it was possible.

Buster walked to Rebecca and held out his hand. She

shot him a look of pure hatred, which softened when he did not pull back. Rebecca reached out and took his hand, letting him lead her away from the bodies.

Marcus O'Brien came over and shook his head at the sight of his boss.

"Dumb son of a bitch," was all O'Brien said. He motioned and got several of his railroad crew over to pick up Colonel Simmons's body.

"What about Newcombe?" Slocum asked.

"Let his men bury him as they see fit."

Slocum tensed. O'Brien was looking at the wagon with the colonel's original coffin. The fighting could break out anew if the construction engineer wanted to press the matter and those remaining guards of Newcombe's wanted to dispute it.

"Get the wagon," O'Brien said. Slocum stepped back, his hand resting on his six-shooter. He waited for an argument but none came. Everyone who had worked for Newcombe was too stunned at the turn of events to protest. Since he had killed Eachin and deprived those guarding the toll road of their second-in-command, no one was willing to step forward.

Two of O'Brien's men got into the wagon with the coffin and drove it slowly through the gate. He directed his men to load the other coffin into the wagon, then put both men's bodies in beside the caskets. O'Brien stared hard at the nearest of Newcombe's guards, then motioned for his driver to start up the steep hill for Bonanza.

"We'll bury them in the town cemetery. Heaven alone knows they'll have enough company there after all that's happened tonight," O'Brien said harshly. The stocky engineer left the toll road guards behind as he walked beside the wagon.

In five minutes only a few men lingered at the gate leading to the toll road. In ten, Slocum stood alone by the barbed wire fence. He heaved a sigh. The fighting was over. But what now?

Slocum made his way up the road but turned to the north, away from the cemetery. He didn't know or much care if O'Brien planned on putting Simmons and New-combe into the ground right away. Slocum had more important business to tend to. He wanted to find Sarah June and make sure she was all right.

The Tons o' Gold Saloon heaved and flapped as if it were some giant beast gasping for breath in the sluggish mountain wind. Slocum pulled back the flap. His heart fell. Sarah June was nowhere to be seen. But a noise behind the bar caused him to go for his six-shooter. He had the Colt out and aimed before Abel had straightened, a bottle of whiskey in his hand.

"Whoa, there, Mr. Slocum. Don't shoot me. I'm only the bartender!"

"Sorry," Slocum said, putting away the six-shooter. "Where's Sarah June?"

"She's off to the mining camp hunting for Bill and Lars. You know them varmints. They're the ones you saved."

"You let her go alone?"

Abel shrugged and said, "She's got a mind of her own, in case you hadn't noticed. She said they was friends and no harm would come. Considerin' all the shooting that's gone on in Bonanza, that struck me as bein' true."

"Do you know where Bill and Lars's claim is?"

"Nope, and Miss Daniels didn't either. That's why she went huntin' them. I reckon she wants them to settle their tab. They're both heavy drinkers and ran up quite a bill."

Slocum left, looking up into the mountains where the majority of the miners dug into the rock hunting for the sulphurets that marked a silver mine. A big strike would have been announced among the tightly clustered mines, so he turned his attention away. In the light of the rising sun, he saw tracks leading to the other side of the mountain, tracks possibly left by Sarah June.

Slocum mounted his horse and slowly followed the trail as it went higher into the hills. The day turned warmer, and he found himself beginning to sweat as the sun beat down on him in spite of the altitude. Not sure he was on Sarah June's trail, he kept riding until he spotted a branch from the main path, if the miserable scratchings in the rock and dirt could be called a main path.

Heading for higher ground, he quickly spotted a solitary mine shaft with a small ramshackle cabin beside it. He made certain his six-shooter was riding easy in its holster as he approached.

"Hello!" he called. No answer. Slocum dismounted and walked around, his nose wrinkling at the acrid smell of chemicals used to test for silver. He found a three-legged stool that had been used as a test stand. Silver glance smeared it. Slocum touched it with his fingers and then held up the dust and crystal to the sunlight.

"So you did hit it big," he said to himself. Slocum looked around, fearing the worst. Men had killed for less wealth than hinted at by the silver streak on his fingers. Sarah June might have walked into a trap and ended up dead as a result. Why should Bill and Lars share such a find with a lady saloon keeper if they could kill her and have it all for themselves?

Slocum swung around, his hand flashing to his six-shooter when he heard metal scraping on rock near the mine shaft leading into the hillside. Bill Parsons struggled from the mouth of the mine lugging two huge burlap bags loaded with ore. Behind him came Lars Dorch, similarly burdened.

"Hold it," Slocum said, aiming for the lead man.

"Slocum!" cried Bill Parsons, startled. "Why are you pointin' that danged thing at me?"

"He's robbin' us, you fool," said Lars Dorch. "Go on, take it all. We got plenty. Steal what you want, Slocum. Go on!"

"Where's—" Slocum cut off his question. A third miner struggled from the mine, dragging yet another bag of ore.

Sarah June Daniels wiped sweat from her eyes and stared at him in wonder. "What are you doing here, John? And why you are pointing that gun at us?"

"I thought you were in trouble."

"Trouble?" Sarah June laughed in delight. "The only trouble we're going to have is figuring out how to spend all this silver!"

"They didn't kidnap you?"

"Why should we?" asked Lars, frowning as he tried to understand what Slocum meant. "Miss Daniels is our partner. We'd never let nuthin' happen to her, especially after she sent you to save us from Eachin."

"We renegotiated a little," she said, dusting off her hands and coming to Slocum. "I didn't think it was fair for me to take more than half, so I insisted we divvy up the take evenly. Each of us gets a third."

Slocum was impressed. Not only was Sarah June honest, so were the two miners.

"I owe you gents an apology," Slocum said. "When I got back to the Tons o' Gold and Sarah June was gone, Abel told me she had gone off hunting for this mine."

"The Sarah June," Bill Parsons said proudly. "We named it after our patron."

"You said you didn't know where the mine was because Bill and Lars wouldn't tell you."

"Not wouldn't," Sarah June said cheerfully. "They just

didn't have a chance. In case you hadn't noticed, Bonanza has been in a bit of an uproar."

"It wasn't until yesterday we figured out how rich this mine really was. We knowed it was good, but not this good 'til we did a complete assay ourselves." Bill said proudly.

Slocum looked at the silvery smear on his fingers and nodded. The strike was a real bonanza.

"If you thought I was in danger, that means trouble really came to a boil in town," Sarah June said. She pressed close to Slocum and said in a low voice so only he could hear, "You came for me because you thought I was in hot water. I like that."

"I should have known you could take care of yourself," Slocum said. "You and your partners have everything under control. I should let you get back to work . . ."

"Don't go runnin' off on account of us, Mr. Slocum," spoke up Lars. "We kin fix you some coffee 'fore you go. Takes paint off wood, but it's 'bout the best you'll find in these parts."

Slocum looked at the barren hills. "It might be the only coffee in these parts."

"That's what I said," Lars joshed. He and Bill dragged their bags down the hill to their cabin, went inside and started fixing some grub to go along with the coffee. This gave Slocum a chance to talk to Sarah June alone.

"Are you going to give up the saloon?" he asked.

"Why would I give up the Tons o' Gold? That's been my dream for, well, forever!"

"You seem to have found your calling here, helping Lars and Bill."

"Oh, this. I wanted to take some samples back to town and was only helping get some of the rock out for them."

"Ore," Slocum corrected. "There's a bunch you don't know about mining."

"And you'll be willing to teach me?" she asked, grinning from ear to ear.

"Reckon the first thing to do is make sure this claim is legal. Since the assay office, along with the records there burned to the ground, you ought to be sure everything is properly registered over in Kennicut. With the colonel's train, you can get over and be back in the same day."

"I don't know, John," the lovely brunette said. "That's mighty complicated. I might need you to help me to be sure it's all done right."

It was Slocum's turn to laugh. He knew when he was being kidded. Sarah June didn't need anyone's help.

"I don't know if you'd want to pay my price for such services," he said.

"And I don't know if you have the stamina to collect," she shot back. Sarah June stood on tiptoe and kissed him fervently. Before anything more could happen between them, Bill shouted for them to come and chow down.

Reluctantly, they went into the small cabin and saw the two miners had prepared quite a spread, including biscuits, preserves, and a rasher of bacon.

"I wanted to keep you here with some decent food 'til you told us everything that'd gone on in Bonanza," Bill said. "We been hidin' out ever since we got grabbed by Eachin. That there town's no place to hang out—'cept in Miss Daniels' saloon, of course," the miner added hastily.

"It's hard to know where to start," Slocum said. When he finished relating all that had happened, Slocum knew there was one more scene to play out.

20

"I don't know if I can, John," Sarah June Daniels said. She backed away from him and looked like a rabbit ready to run.

"It'll be the end of the feud," Slocum told her.

"I can't believe that. Their fathers fought like mad dogs. They will, too."

"There's no harm going out to the cemetery for the services," he pointed out. He looked around the Tons o' Gold Saloon. Nobody was here but Abel, who polished new shot glasses brought in by train from Denver through Kennicut.

"I want to be sure Bill and Lars are all right," she said, obviously hunting for any excuse to get out of going to the Simmons and Newcombe funerals.

"They won't be back for a spell since the train is *here* in Bonanza," Slocum pointed out. "They can't get back until the train makes another round-trip and that won't happen until after the funeral."

"They won't leave," Sarah June said positively. "That harpy will stay."

Slocum knew Sarah June's problem with Rebecca, and

it had nothing to do with the fight between Malcolm New-combe and Colonel Simmons. It had everything to do with Slocum formerly working for the Colorado Grand Mountain Railroad.

Formerly.

He had not been paid the fabulous salary promised and doubted he would see a red cent of it. Slocum didn't care. Sarah June had promised him the gambling concession in the other tent again. A month or two running it in a boom-town like Bonanza once word of the huge silver strike made by Bill Parsons and Lars Dorch got out would make Slocum rich. Not as rich as Sarah June because of her share in the Sarah June Mine or from the Tons o' Gold, but rich enough.

He looked at the lovely brunette and knew there were other reasons to stick around and buck the tiger that had nothing to do with money.

"Oh, very well. Be sure you have your six-shooter loaded and ready," Sarah June said anxiously.

Slocum patted his trusty six-gun, then extended his arm for her to take. They left the saloon and walked the length of the main street. Most of the buildings had been burned down in the fighting but some were already being rebuilt. The sound of hammers hitting nails quieted as the citizens made their way out to the cemetery south of town.

"They'll pick up the feud again. I feel it in my bones," Sarah June muttered as they entered the cemetery. Bonanza had hardly been in existence long enough to fill up more than a row of graves, but the recent fighting had more than doubled the population. One grave even sported a Masonic emblem, showing the fraternal society had members in Bo-nanza.

Slocum saw how Buster Newcombe and Rebecca Sim-mons stood at opposite sides of the wagon that had brought both their fathers out to this desolate hill. It sur-

prised him that Rebecca wanted the colonel buried here
rather than in Denver amid a big social event. The burial
was happening so fast even the *Rocky Mountain News* had
not had time to send out a reporter.

"Where'd they find a minister?" Sarah June asked in a
low voice.

Slocum shook his head. Silver and gold strikes brought
in a flood of eager prospectors from all backgrounds. The
man holding the Bible and looking solemn might have
been hunting for silver glance only hours before being
tapped to perform the burial service.

The minister started his baleful recitation of the two
men's deaths, but Slocum found his attention focused on
Rebecca and Buster. They stood apart and yet they . . .
weren't.

"So we commit these mortal remains to the ground in
the hope of resurrection," the minister finished. Men
grabbed the handles on the sides of the coffins and put
them into the ground in adjoining graves.

"Which coffin is which?" whispered Sarah June. "Did
the colonel get his original casket?"

Slocum could not tell. He had not been paying that
much attention to the dead. As always, the living were
more interesting.

Buster and Rebecca finally stepped up and paid their
last respects to their fathers, then turned and began arguing.

"Here we go again," Sarah June said. "They'll destroy
the town with a new feud."

"Wait," Slocum said. While the brunette might be right,
he read the two in a different way.

Rebecca turned, cleared her throat and said loudly, "Let
the bloodshed be ended with our fathers. Buster and I want
to announce that a second Colorado Grand Mountain Railroad spur line will come to Bonanza—through the canyon

where the Newcombe toll road now runs. We intend to make it full-scale, standard gauge, to better link with major lines."

"That means we'll get miners from all over Colorado now!" Sarah June exclaimed.

Slocum said nothing. Laying track along the toll road—the former toll road—would be quickly done since there weren't any obstacles like Knife Canyon to overcome. It also meant the narrow-gauge line from Kennicut would quickly fall into disuse, dooming Kennicut once more. But that was the way of the boomtown. Sudden surges up and falls as rapid.

Slocum wondered what Marcus O'Brien thought about his fine work crossing the deadly canyon being for nothing. O'Brien seemed excited at the prospect of laying standard track for a change. He was a man who looked forward, never back.

"I never thought they would come to agree on anything," Sarah June said, still excited at what this meant for Bonanza. "Buster has to know the toll road will be worthless with a railroad running down his canyon."

"Further," Rebecca Simmons went on, "I am naming Buster Newcombe to the board of directors of the Colorado Grand Mountain Railroad."

Sarah June's jaw dropped. Slocum waited for the rest of what he knew to be coming. He was not disappointed.

"And I am pleased to announce that Miss Simmons has agreed to marry me," Buster Newcombe cut in.

For a moment there was only silence, then a cheer went up. Slocum took Sarah June's arm and steered her away from the cemetery and back into Bonanza, a Bonanza that would suddenly double and double again in population before the end of summer.

"We've got a lot of work to do to get ready for the land rush," Sarah June said, more excited than ever.

"They won't be here for a while yet," Slocum said, looking at the woman. "We can take a little time for ourselves."

Sarah June smiled and moved closer to him. "You're right, John, but you always are!"

Watch for

VALLEY OF SKULLS

274th novel in the exciting SLOCUM series
from Jove

Coming in December!

JAKE LOGAN
TODAY'S HOTTEST ACTION WESTERN!

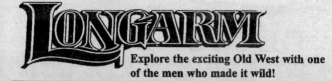

Explore the exciting Old West with one of the men who made it wild!